"What does yo
being in a dangerous place?" Sophie asked.

"It means that she has a good idea where the leak is coming from and that it's from a source that leaves us all vulnerable."

"So where could we hide where we won't be found while they fix the situation?"

"I have no idea."

Aiden was a man who liked to be in control. But he had absolutely no control over this whole case anymore. His cover was blown. He had no backup. And he was the only person standing between the sisters and those who would kill them. Whatever actions he took could literally mean life or death for them.

Shifting his eyes to Sophie, he saw something in her bright green gaze that he hadn't anticipated seeing. Trust. Despite all she'd been through, this woman had chosen to put her trust and her faith in him.

And that terrified him more than anything else.

Dana R. Lynn grew up in Illinois. She met her husband at a wedding and told her parents she'd met the man she was going to marry. Nineteen months later, they were married. Today, they live in rural Pennsylvania with their three children and a variety of animals. In addition to writing, she works as a teacher for the deaf and hard of hearing and is active in her church.

Books by Dana R. Lynn

Love Inspired Suspense

Amish Country Justice

Plain Target
Plain Retribution
Amish Christmas Abduction
Amish Country Ambush
Amish Christmas Emergency
Guarding the Amish Midwife
Hidden in Amish Country
Plain Refuge

Amish Witness Protection

Amish Haven

Visit the Author Profile page at Harlequin.com.

PLAIN REFUGE

DANA R. LYNN

LOVE INSPIRED SUSPENSE
INSPIRATIONAL ROMANCE

LOVE INSPIRED® SUSPENSE
INSPIRATIONAL ROMANCE

ISBN-13: 978-1-335-40285-1

Plain Refuge

Copyright © 2020 by Dana Roae

This edition published by arrangement with Harlequin Books S.A.

For questions and comments about the quality of this book, please contact us at CustomerService@Harlequin.com.

Love Inspired
22 Adelaide St. West, 40th Floor
Toronto, Ontario M5H 4E3, Canada
www.Harlequin.com

Printed in U.S.A.

From the rising of the sun unto the going down
of the same the Lord's name is to be praised.
–Psalms 113:3

To my niece, Evelyn. You are a blessing and we love you.

ONE

"Are you close to making an arrest, Lieutenant?"

"Hold on a second." Aiden Forster glanced around, scanning his surroundings to ensure his call was private. He pretended to be messing with his helmet while he waited for a woman jogging with her dog to go by. Then he lifted his head and glanced around again. No one was in sight. Good. He raised his cell phone to his ear, making sure to keep his voice low. Just in case there was someone lurking in the shadows. He knew all too well that information in the wrong hands could be deadly. He'd been a lieutenant in the Narcotics division long enough to witness some routine operations go horribly wrong without warning. Police work could be brutal. Sometimes devastating.

"Close, ma'am. I hope to be able to have enough to move on within the next two weeks." He chose his words carefully. Mentioning evidence or the chief's title were not words that would be misinterpreted if overheard.

Please, Lord, let me be telling the truth.

He had pulled over to take the call from his chief, knowing she was getting anxious to have this case over and done with. He was in full agreement with her there. The movies had made undercover work seem so cool, but the reality was the work was grueling, taking its toll emotionally and spiritually. After being on this operation for six months, he could feel it wearing him down. Every night, he pulled out his Bible, trying to build up his strength for the next day.

For nearly half a year, Aiden had played the part of Adam Steele, a hardened hired killer and drug dealer. His rap sheet was all fiction, created to give him a reputation for ruthlessness. His chief had also allowed several "leaks" to the press about him.

All of it paid off when he'd been contacted by Phillip Larson to do a few jobs on the side. Mostly drug related. It wasn't enough. The chief knew that Larson was involved with running drugs in the area. What they needed was proof to link him to cartels coming across the border, as well as two contract hits on politicians fighting against the cartels. Up to this moment, Aiden hadn't learned anything that could connect Larson to anything larger than some minor drug trafficking. Today could be a huge break in the case. Larson had invited him to his house for a private meeting with an important client.

He just had to play his part for a little bit longer.

It was getting harder to continue the charade. The evil he faced, indeed a part of each and every day, was slowly breaking him apart.

What really terrified him was the way the line between right and wrong seemed to be blurring. Not that he didn't still understand what was right. But he was aware on an alarming level of the desensitization occurring in himself.

He had to hold on for just a little bit longer. If he could get what he needed, he could pull free. Then he'd go on a long vacation to recuperate. He'd earned it.

"I'll give you the two weeks, but it might be necessary to pull you out sooner if you can't get it." Her strong voice with its subtle Midwest accent pulled him back to the conversation.

When he started to protest, Chief Daniels interrupted him. "I'm serious, Aiden. You're one of my best lieutenants, but I'm concerned about your state of mind."

So was he. As much as he wanted to find justice and put Phillip Larson behind bars, he was beginning to wonder if he was losing himself in the dark world he'd been inhabiting. Still, the thought of giving in and allowing Larson to remain free to kill and harm those who got in his way made his teeth ache.

He couldn't do it. His own partner had been a victim of Larson's evil reach. Tim had gotten an anonymous tip about a major deal going down. He had called it in and requested backup. Aiden had gotten there to aid his partner as soon as he could, but it wasn't fast enough. Tim had been ambushed, killed with a single shot to the back of his head. He owed it to Tim to end this. Then he could put his guilt at not arriving in time behind him. And it would be nice to be able to tell Tim's widow that her husband's killer had been brought to justice.

"I'll get him, ma'am. Then I'll be done with this cover for good."

And, hopefully, he'd never need to go undercover again.

"See that you do. Are you on your way to him now?"

"Yep. He called a meeting. Not sure what about exactly. All I know is he said an important client would be meeting us at his house. And not to be late, if I knew what was good for me."

"Keep me posted, Lieutenant."

He ended the call and put the phone back into the zippered pocket of his leather jacket. Pushing his helmet back onto his head, he kicked the motorcycle to life. The one part of this gig he enjoyed was being able to ride his motorcycle every day. The chief had allowed it because she felt it fit in with the image he was cultivating. When people looked at him, they saw a ruthless man willing to do anything if the price was right.

Larson had left his garage open. That wasn't like him. Was he expecting someone else? Aiden was puzzled. He'd never met anyone more emphatic—almost fanatical—about privacy. While most people wouldn't think anything about leaving a garage door open, he knew that Phillip Larson would be furious that anyone walking by could look and see even that little bit of his life exposed.

Keeping to their established protocol, Aiden ignored the open garage and drove his bike around the block, using the alley to pull in behind the house, where his bike wouldn't be visible from the street. He removed his helmet and placed it on the bike, then he covered the motorcycle with the tarp that was left for that purpose.

Aiden slipped his sunglasses on and strode toward the house. His stomach muscles tightened. He forced his shoulders to relax. He was Adam Steele now, not Aiden Forster. Adam Steele, one of Phillip Larson's trusted associates. Larson had no idea that some of the information he'd supplied, as well as some of the business he'd drummed up, had been carefully orchestrated with the cooperation of his colleagues at the police station. A bitter taste filled his mouth. The adrenaline rush he'd first experienced after he'd been chosen for the undercover operation had died out months ago. When this case was closed and Larson was in prison, he'd be released from this identity that he'd grown to despise.

Adam Steele was ruthless, a man who had no compunction about committing any number of felonies. At least, that's what Phillip thought.

When the time was right, Aiden would take great pleasure in letting the man know just who had been working with him for months.

At this very moment, though, he needed to get his head in the game. Phillip Larson was a shark. If he scented any weakness or hint of deceit, he'd be out for blood. Rolling his shoulders one last time, Aiden took in a deep breath and slipped into the persona of Adam Steele.

He approached the house by the back door, as he'd been instructed to do. The low rumble of an engine halted him before he entered the house. Someone was pulling up the driveway.

That was not in the plan that Phillip had told him on the phone last night. No one else was supposed to be at the house until after their business was concluded.

He knew Phillip would not have changed plans without telling him first. The man was very rigid. He liked to control every moment and didn't like surprises. Anything that affected his image or how his business was managed was methodically planned out and handled.

Aiden changed direction. Keeping close to the outer garage wall, he made his way around the side of the building to where he had a clear view of the driveway.

An unfamiliar vehicle was rolling up in plain sight. Not good. Maybe whoever it was would leave quickly. Maybe it was just someone who'd gone the wrong direction and needed to turn around. The car halted and shifted into Park.

There seemed to be two people in the car. Aiden couldn't get a good view of the girl sitting in the back seat, but he could clearly see the woman in the front. Dark sunglasses hid her eyes, and her hair was pulled back into a thick ponytail high on the back of her head. It was a bright coppery red. Oval face, high cheekbones. Her mouth was drawn into a frown.

She looked familiar. Had he met her? He didn't think so. His memory was sharp. No way he'd forget that face.

A second later, it clicked. Phillip had mentioned that his niece was coming over later. Aiden checked the time on his phone. She was early. Really early. He bit off the frustrated exclamation that rose to his lips as she turned off the engine. Aiden didn't know that much about Phillip's family, but he did know that his boss wouldn't let any affection he may have had for them ruin a business deal. And listening to him talk about his family, Aiden knew Phillip did not harbor much feeling other than disgust for most of his family.

This had all the warning signs of an impending disaster.

If Phillip wasn't ready for her, she was as good as dead. And so was her passenger.

Aiden couldn't let that happen. The only thing standing between the beautiful young woman who'd had the misfortune of coming at the wrong time and murder was him. To save her meant he'd have to think fast. It might even mean that his cover, and all the months of intense observation, evidence collection and brutal police work would be destroyed in one instant.

There was no decision.

Aiden could not stand by and let an innocent person die. With a quick prayer for all their safety, he waited. If he could get them out without blowing his cover, he would. If this situation blew up, though, he'd be ready to step in.

No matter the cost.

"I'll just be a minute," Sophie Larson signed to her sister, Celine. "Are you okay staying in the car?"

The sassy twelve-year-old rolled her eyes before turning her attention back to her phone, her mouth turned down in a sullen frown. Sophie noticed that the preteen had removed her cochlear implant processors from both sides of her head. They were no doubt shoved into the backpack on the seat beside her. Without them, her sister wouldn't hear anything, including speech. Most likely a deliberate choice. Celine was mad that Sophie was selling their parents' house and taking her to live with Sophie in Chicago. She had refused to even sit in the front seat next to her older sister. Sophie shrugged, determined not to take it personally. That was a battle she'd let go until later, when she had more time and wasn't feeling so overwhelmed.

Sophie bit back a sigh. Her sister was grieving the loss of their parents and seventeen-year-old brother, Brian. They both were. The shock of losing them in a random break-in hadn't yet settled in, even though they'd been gone for almost a month. If Celine had been home, she probably would have died, too. Fortunately, she was away at the Western Pennsylvania School for the Deaf at the time of the break-in.

Guilt tunneled through Sophie. She was thirteen years older than Celine. By the time the younger girl was eight, Sophie had already moved out and was living three states away in Chicago. She'd been busy building her career with a rapidly growing marketing company. They might have been sisters, but she felt she barely knew the younger girl. For the past four years, they'd only seen each other when she came back to Pennsylvania for the holidays.

The sooner she handled the mess with her uncle Phillip and got back on the road toward their parents' home, the better. Sophie had toyed with the idea of putting the house on the market, but for the sake of her sister, she'd decided to hold on to it. It was paid off and left to her in her parents' will. Celine wasn't happy about moving to Chicago, but Sophie felt it was the best thing to do.

She gathered a thick stack of envelopes, glad Celine had no interest in accompanying her.

Uncle Phillip might have been their dad's brother, but he made Sophie nervous for reasons she couldn't explain. His wide smile and hearty greetings always felt a tad overdone. And the brown eyes that had been so warm and loving in the face of her father were shifty on her uncle. Her father and Uncle Phillip had not gotten along, so she had only ever seen the man a few times a year growing up.

He was still family, she reminded herself. At least she didn't have to contest him for guardianship of Celine. And she would have. If anyone was going to raise her sister, it would be her.

But first she had some papers to drop off. Her father had left the house and property to Sophie and her siblings, but he had a few investments he was leaving his brother. She had some statements and files that should be handed over. The lawyer had mentioned that Talon Hill, Ohio, wasn't that far out of her way. Really, only a little jaunt over the Pennsylvania-Ohio border. All she wanted to do was return home. She knew, however, that she would probably never see her uncle again. Out of respect for her father, she'd agreed. She glanced at her watch. She was thirty minutes early. Her uncle, she knew, was a stickler for punctuality. He wouldn't appreciate her being late—or early. It would interfere with his schedule. She bit her lip, gnawing on it while she considered her options. She could sit in the car and wait. But her sister was bound to become difficult. Sophie was doing her best to help Celine cope with the changes in her life. A quick glance in the mirror showed her sister was still engrossed in her device. Who knew how long it would be until she needed Sophie's attention again?

Abruptly Sophie grabbed the envelopes and opened the car door. Her uncle would have to deal with the inconvenience. Celine was her priority. Swiftly, before she could change her mind, she strode up the drive and let herself into the indoor porch. It was neat as a pin, almost uncomfortably tidy.

She snorted. Just because her own apartment was cluttered, it didn't mean there was anything inherently wrong with not having knickknacks and books taking up every empty space.

She rang the bell and heard the chimes echoing inside the house. Nothing happened. Annoyed, she shoved her sunglasses up on top of her head. He knew she was on the way. Was he deliberately letting her wait to punish her for showing up early? Surely not.

Turning her body so she could see the car, she shifted the papers to the other hand, preparing to ring the bell again. She stopped.

Leaning closer to the door, she listened. Someone inside the house was shouting.

The urge to leave the papers on the porch and run swept over her.

But she had promised the lawyer she'd hand these directly to Uncle Phillip.

Her uncle's voice yelled out again.

Was he calling for her to enter? What if he needed

her? Images of her relative possibly suffering from a heart attack or maybe injured stalled the impulse to leave. Her parents had not raised her to ignore those in need. Pressing her lips together, she shoved the door open and stepped into the house.

Her eyes blinked in the dimmer light of the hall. She had forgotten how dark this old house was.

Sophie had opened her mouth to call out, when a different voice yelled.

She knew that voice. Cash Wellman, a young man who worked with Uncle Phillip. She'd talked with him a time or two in the past. He had asked her out, and she had politely declined. He seemed like a nice enough man, but Sophie had long ago decided that she would not date a man who didn't share her faith.

"You've disappointed me, Cash."

Her uncle's voice again. Now she could tell he wasn't injured. His voice was harsh. Angry.

"I'll make it up to you, sir. You'll see." Cash's voice sounded weird. Like he was terrified. Why would he fear her uncle?

"You'd better."

She shivered. Phillip's voice became smooth with a menacing edge. "I have quite a large sum of money riding on this deal. If these weapons don't reach the correct hands by Saturday, my client will go seek out another supplier. I can't let that happen."

Sophie shoved a fist into her mouth to hold in the horrified cry that bubbled in her throat. Were they actually talking about selling weapons? Her uncle sold insurance. Or at least that's what she had always been led to believe.

Suddenly her innocent errand reeked of danger.

She needed to leave. Now.

Spinning, she slammed into someone. Hard, muscular arms grabbed on to her. To steady her or to imprison her?

"Sophie."

She trembled from head to feet at the sound of her uncle behind her. The man holding her stepped back.

"Ah, Adam. You're early, as well."

The dark-haired man she had slammed into gave a sharp nod, his cold eyes zeroing in on Phillip's face. She couldn't breathe. Spots danced in front of her eyes. She'd never been so terrified. Celine! Her sister was so close, alone and vulnerable. What would happen if she decided to come and find Sophie?

"Is there a problem, Mr. Larson?" Adam rumbled, his voice soft and deep. There was no emotion in his voice. He could have walked in on a picnic.

Sophie found her voice. "Uncle Phillip, I just came by to give you these papers. So, if you'll excuse me—"

Phillip chuckled. It was a humorless sound. "Just like that? Ah, Sophie. You know that I can't have that. You have walked into a mess. I can't have you telling tales. Adam," he said, his cold eyes assessing the man, "you've been valuable. I can't seem to trust my associate Cash here to deal with the delicate details."

The man called Adam stepped over to her and grabbed her by the elbow. The barrel of a gun poked into her ribs. "I'll take care of it for you, sir. For a fee, of course."

Her uncle nodded. "Of course. Of course. Not here, obviously. I have too much at stake to allow anything to happen on these premises."

"You can leave it to me. No one will ever find the body."

Before she could blink, Sophie was being dragged outside. The nudge of the gun in her side helped keep her under control. She knew that she needed to stay focused so she could rescue Celine.

"Walk so the neighbors won't get suspicious," her captor growled in her ear.

Her car was still running. She could see her sister, still sitting in the back seat. Celine looked up, and her eyes flared wide with alarm. Adam opened the passenger-side door and pushed her toward it.

"Get into the driver's seat, and don't try anything funny."

How could she get out of this without Celine being hurt? Her whole body shook as she obeyed. She slid across the seat and climbed over the console, aware of the man folding himself into the passenger seat. For a brief moment, Sophie contemplated scooting out the driver's-side door, but then what? She couldn't run down the driveway to the street and leave the man in the car with her sister. No, she'd have to wait and pray for an opportunity. Her kidnapper slammed his door closed and ordered her to drive. She shifted into Drive and continued along the U-shaped driveway until she was back on the main road. No one was around. The small hope that she'd see someone outside who might be able to help them faded. A trickle of sweat rolled down the back of her neck. Her eyes met the terrified hazel gaze of her sister in the rearview mirror. All the color had fled Celine's young face.

Keep still, she mouthed, praying Celine would read her lips. To her credit, the twelve-year-old kept her cool. She nodded, her mouth trembling, then sank down against the back seat.

Sophie swallowed hard, her blood pumping in her ears. She ordered herself to stay calm.

"Turn left."

She followed the man's directions, all the while desperately searching and praying for an escape. Movement in the back seat caught her attention. Her eyes met Celine's in the mirror again. Her sister had put her processors back on. Fiercely, Sophie clamped down on the hysteria rising up inside her. She couldn't afford to panic. Not if they were going to get out of this alive.

Adam what's-his-name reached into his pocket and removed a cell phone. As he moved, his leather jacket shifted, giving her a clear view of the gun strapped to his side.

She shuddered at their precarious position. No matter how she thought about it, she couldn't see a way out of this mess. This man, Adam, was leading them to their deaths. At her uncle's orders. All of her goals in life shrank to one single prayer.

Please Lord. Protect my sister.

TWO

Aiden could smell the fear emanating off the woman beside him. As much as he hated being the cause of her fear, he couldn't risk breaking his cover. Not yet. Not until they had put enough distance between themselves and Larson.

When had this job become so complicated? He'd been so close to getting what he needed. The man responsible for his best friend and fellow lieutenant's death had no idea that one of his trusted men was really an undercover police lieutenant working on locking him away for the rest of his life. Seeing Phillip Larson behind bars had become Aiden's reason for getting up in the morning. It was the only reason he was able to stomach being thrust into the underbelly of the crime ring in Talon Hill, Ohio, for the past six months. All of his hard work, all of his sacrifices. Gone. And all because of the pretty redhead seated inches away from him.

She couldn't have known that showing up early would result in such disastrous consequences. Still, the tide of resentment that rolled through him had him gritting his teeth. He thrust the emotion aside. She and her sister were the innocents in all this.

Despite hoping that everything would work out, he'd known the moment he had walked into the house and seen her standing there, horror written on every inch of her face, that she had heard too much. The moment she'd run into him, he'd recognized that his time was up. He'd had to act fast to save her and himself. He'd steeled himself for action, knowing that he needed to find a way to get them both out of the house.

And then Phillip had walked out and seen her. In that instant, Aiden had read her death in the other man's eyes. The fact that she was his niece made no difference. Money came before everything in the world he'd entered. Including family.

Fortunately, Phillip was very conscious of his reputation. He enjoyed entertaining in the privacy of his home. Which meant that he wouldn't have wanted anyone to kill her on the premises. No, Phillip would not have wanted that mess in his home. Which gave Aiden time to act without suspicion. But only for now. Suspicion would fall on him soon enough.

It didn't matter now. He was out of the game, and someone else would need to go in and clean up the mess he was leaving behind. Hearing a slight sniffle in the back seat, he turned his head and saw the young girl, pale and trembling. He'd been so anxious to get the woman out of the house and away from her murderous uncle, he'd not paid too much attention to the girl.

His phone buzzed in his pocket. Grabbing it, he looked at the display and hesitated. He needed to answer, but any hope of maintaining his cover until they were farther away would most likely die with it. It couldn't be helped. He sighed and answered the call.

"Forster."

"Your GPS shows that you're moving away from the Larson house, Lieutenant," Chief Daniels commented, a question in her smooth voice. "I thought you were supposed to be there for a meeting."

"Yes, ma'am. There was a complication." He cast a glance over at the woman driving the car, her hands clenched on the steering wheel. She was listening to every word, her mouth tight and her brow shiny with perspiration, even though the car was cool with the air-conditioning humming.

"Complication? Explain," the chief rapped out.

"Hold on a second." He pulled the phone away from his mouth briefly. "Turn onto the interstate."

She didn't answer as she flipped on the blinker. Her hands weren't shaking as much as they had been. The color was coming back in her face. She shot him an intense glance rife with confusion and curiosity. Interesting. The fear seemed to be draining from her like a tire slowly deflating. She was probably figuring out that he didn't really plan on killing her.

"Who are you talking to, Forster?" Chief Daniels brought him back to the moment.

"Larson's nieces showed up at his house this morning at an inopportune moment. I'm not sure how much they know, but he wasn't happy with their presence."

The older sister flicked her eyes in his direction again, eyebrows raised. Now he was positive she was connecting the dots. Hope flashed in those hazel eyes. He nodded at her, hoping she would understand that he wasn't really the enemy.

"Describe unhappy, Forster."

"He ordered me to take care of them," he reported.

A soft cry came from behind him. The younger sister. He winced. Ouch. She'd been so quiet he'd forgotten about her.

The older sister lifted her right hand and made several deliberate motions to her sister. Was that sign language? The girl sat back. Lifting his visor, he peered at her in his mirror, noticing what looked like taupe-colored behind-the-ear hearing aids on both her ears. Except these didn't look like any hearing aids he'd ever seen before. These were connected to a wire and flat circular objects that stuck to the sides of her head. And there were no ear molds. How had he missed them earlier?

The young girl wilted back against the seat. Whatever the redhead said had obviously reassured her sister. Just how much could the girl hear and understand?

"I'll send a crew to assess the damage. See if we can get a tap or something to check if your cover's been blown," Chief Daniels said.

"I'm going to assume it has. When I don't return with proof that I have carried out his request, Larson's bound to send men after us." He looked over at the woman beside him.

"I'd tell you to bring the civilians in, but we've had some sensitive information reach the wrong people in the past two weeks. You need to find a place and hole up until we find out who's doing this."

A mole? Seriously? Could this day get any worse?

"I will, Chief." He grimaced, knowing his cover was officially blown. Well, he couldn't change it. "First, though, I need to return to my loft and gather the intel I've collected on Larson. We might have enough to go to the DA with what I have."

"Do you need me to send another lieutenant out to get the women? I can send Baylor."

He thought about it for a few seconds. Baylor was as solid as they came. Still, the time factor was a concern.

"We're in crunch time. I need to go now before Larson sends someone there to trash my place. By the time another unit arrives, it might be too late. In fact, I'd just about guarantee it."

The redhead—Sophie, he reminded himself—sat straight in her seat. Casting a glance her way, he could practically see the pieces coming together in her mind.

Chief Daniels was silent for a moment. When she replied, he could hear the reluctance in her voice. Chief Daniels was a practical woman. She might not like the situation, but she would move forward with what could be done. "Very well, Lieutenant. I'm relying on you to keep yourself and those women out of trouble."

"Understood. I'll keep sharp. Once Larson figures out what's what, there's no way he'd let me walk away alive if he can stop it. Not after the things I've seen and heard."

Gathering intel? Chief? Bubbles of hope rose in Sophie, and her suspicion was confirmed. Adam wasn't really who her uncle thought he was. With this knowledge came the comfort that he wasn't planning on killing them, even though her uncle had ordered their deaths. She was still shocked at how casually he'd tried to dispose of her and Celine.

"Who are you?" Sophie whispered when he put his phone away. It was easier to breathe now that she had decided he wasn't going to shoot them and drop their bodies off a cliff somewhere.

The man, Adam or Forster or whatever his real name was, didn't respond right away. Instead, he turned his head away to stare out the window. She was getting ready to ask again when he turned back to her, snaring her eyes with his dark ones.

"My name is Aiden Forster. I'm a lieutenant with the Talon Hill Police Department. We've had Phillip Larson under investigation for various crimes, including murder, drug smuggling and selling illegal weapons, for over a year now. I was undercover to gather enough evidence to prosecute the man."

A lieutenant. All the bits and pieces from the conversation she had overheard clicked into place. How close had he been to arresting Uncle Phillip? Another chilling thought entered her mind.

"Uncle Phillip—he'll be after us. He knows us, has access to so much information about Celine and me. I don't know what we can do."

"Sophie, would he really hurt us? His own family?" Celine sat forward in her seat, situating herself so she could read lips better. If they were stopped, she could face her sister to make communication easier.

Sophie winced at the question. Now that she was

·

wearing her implants, Celine could hear most of their conversation. She was able to catch the rest through reading lips. She hated that her baby sister was having to deal with this horror and betrayal. She'd been through too much already. They both had. But she didn't shy away from answering. What good would it do? Celine was an intelligent girl who had clearly connected the dots.

"Yeah, he'd hurt us. I don't know everything he's got going on, but it's bad." All she had to do was visualize the cold expression on her uncle's face at the house to know with bone-deep certainty that he would do that, and more, to protect himself.

Beside her, Aiden shifted so that he was partially turned on the seat. Did he realize her sister would benefit from seeing his face?

"Look, I have to get the evidence I've been collecting for the past few months, then I'm going to get you to a safe place while I help shut down this operation."

"Why aren't we just going to go to the police?" Sophie demanded, a sharp edge to her voice.

He seemed to hesitate for a moment. "There have been several instances when information has gotten into the wrong hands," he finally stated.

She digested this morsel of intelligence, startled. "There's a leak? Who?"

He shook his head. "We have no idea who. I don't even know if it's definite that it's from inside the department. But until I find out, I don't think it would be safe to take you there."

Sophie shook her head. This was stuff right out of

a bad soap opera. Her uncle was really a crime boss of some kind, the man he ordered to kill them was an undercover cop, and there was a mole somewhere. Unbelievable. Any minute now she'd wake up from this nightmare.

She opened her mouth to tell him so, when a ding from the dashboard distracted her.

"What was that?" Aiden asked, leaning near her to peer at the dashboard gauges.

Great. And now the low-fuel light was on.

"We're going to have to stop for gas." She bit her lip. As much as she didn't want to keep driving without direction, she suspected they hadn't driven far enough away from Uncle Phillip to satisfy their captor-turned-rescuer. Daring to cast a quick glance Aiden's way, she saw a deep frown settle on his face.

"I'd like to get a little farther down the road before we stop. But, eventually, we're going to have to find a way to switch vehicles anyway."

"Wait…what?"

"Sophie, your uncle is bound to realize that I am helping you when I don't return. He knows your vehicle. It's only a matter of time before someone comes searching for us."

"Can you call him or something?" She thought frantically. "Call him and tell him you took care of us. And maybe you need to dispose of our bodies or something? You know…stall for time."

"Ugh." Celine's face had paled. "That's really gruesome."

Aiden flashed Sophie a look. Was that respect she saw?

"Sorry, kid. I know that it sounds awful, but your sister has a good idea. That might give us a little more wiggle room."

"My name's Celine. Not kid."

If her sister was feeling feisty enough to argue about her name, it was a good sign. Still, the whole mess had to be freaking her out.

"Celine," Aiden corrected himself, pulling his cell phone back out of his pocket. "I don't need to tell you ladies to be silent while I make this call."

Celine flopped back against the seat, the epitome of an offended teen. If the situation wasn't so deadly, Sophie might have been tempted to smile.

She didn't, though. Sophie kept driving, her heart pounding as he made the call. How were his hands so steady? She knew he was a police lieutenant, but she couldn't imagine having the ability to deal with what he did so calmly. Her stomach clenched tight. The volume was up enough that she could hear Uncle Phillip's phone ringing. And then it wasn't. Queasiness gripped her as she heard his distant voice answer. She couldn't make out the words he said, but just realizing that the man she'd known since she was born was holding the phone on the other end, waiting to hear that she was dead, was too twisted for words.

"It's done." Aiden clipped out, the menace in his tone startling her. Even though she knew he was acting, ice filled her veins.

What did it do to someone's mind, to their soul, to have to live that close to evil day after day? To immerse oneself in the world of crime enough to make people like Phillip Larson trust them?

She sent a brief prayer for him, for all of them, winging up to God. She said a special prayer that her impulsive sister would remember to remain silent. While Celine would never deliberately put them in danger, sometimes she forgot how much her sister was able to hear when she was wearing her processors.

Then she tuned back in to Aiden's side of the conversation. He glanced over and caught her glance. After a brief hesitation, he turned the volume up slightly on his phone. Her eyes widened. She could make out her uncle's smooth voice on the other end of the line. Thankfully, it wasn't loud enough for Celine to hear what their only living male relative was saying.

Unfortunately, Sophie was able to hear every single terrifying word.

THREE

"Good. I'm glad you were able to complete your errand," Phillip responded, a slight emphasis on the word *errand*. The satisfaction oozing through the phone was chilling. The man who was supposed to love them was a creep. She was slightly comforted by the look of pure disgust on Aiden's face. He appeared to share her opinion. "Were there any issues?"

"Nope. Everything went smooth." She shivered. Aiden was a cop, working to bring Phillip down and make him pay for his crimes. She was grateful for the knowledge; otherwise, she would have been scared to death. His stony expression alone would have terrified her.

No. If he hadn't been a cop, she would be dead already. What kind of strength did it take to do such a job, day in and day out?

She leaned in closer as Phillip spoke.

"Good. Very good. When you get back, I have another job for you."

That got a response. Aiden scowled and pulled the

phone away to glare at it briefly. None of that was reflected in his voice when he replied.

"Sure. I just need to get rid of some stuff. My payment for the errand?"

"It will be processed as soon as you return with a receipt." Phillip ended the call.

"Did he say you needed to show him a receipt?" Sophie cringed at her shrill tone. She hadn't thought she could be any more shocked than she was.

Celine leaned forward again.

He nodded. "Yeah, he's going to want proof. That's how he works."

"What kind of proof would you provide?" Celine asked.

Sophie held her breath.

Aiden grimaced. "I'm not sure yet. I'll figure something out."

She wasn't buying it. He knew. He was being heroic and trying to protect her sister from the grisly details. She appreciated it. Still, knowing what was going on could keep them from making some mistakes.

Sophie eyed her sister in the mirror. The preteen shrugged and settled down again, returning her attention to her phone.

"Aiden," she whispered, checking the mirror to be sure Celine didn't pick up her voice.

"Yeah?" He raised his eyebrows.

"What kind of proof?"

He stared at her for ten seconds. She bit her lip, waiting. Nodding, he raked his hand through his short dark hair and blew out a breath, hard. "I will show him a picture of your bodies."

"Our bodies!" she shrieked.

Celine's head shot up. "What's going on? Sophie?"

"Sorry. Nothing." She waited for her sister to insist on knowing what they were talking about. Instead, Celine shrugged and leaned her head against the seat. Within two minutes her eyes were closed.

"What do you mean, our bodies?" Sophie hissed, keeping her eyes on her sister.

"We'd fake it, obviously. I've never actually killed anyone for him. I'm certainly not about to start now." He smirked. She felt like an idiot. He straightened and pointed out the window. "Take the next exit and then we'll head back to my place."

"Doesn't my uncle know where you live?"

"Yes and no. He knows where Adam supposedly lives. I'm not going back there. Where we're going is my base for this operation. No one has been there except for me. Only my chief and I know about it. For now. Once I'm found out, Phillip and his henchmen will tear the town apart searching for me."

He took her through back roads and alleys. They finally came to a building that had seen better days. It appeared to be an old recreational complex of some sort. Some of the windows were boarded up. Several bare patches on the roof, where shingles had fallen off, were visible from the ground. It was a depressing structure.

Celine woke up as they parked near the back doorway. Aiden opened his door and climbed out. When Sophie opened her door, he whipped his head around and glared. "You should stay here."

"Not on your life," she retorted. "We stick together. If someone came looking for you here, we'd be alone. You have the only gun."

She thought he would argue. Celine's door opened and his jaw snapped shut. "Fine. Keep close."

The outside door swung open with a high-pitched creak. Sophie flinched. Aiden didn't react at all. Holding her breath, she ducked in through the opening and found, to her surprise, that the interior of the building was fairly clean. She'd expected to find dust, debris and cobwebs. While there were a few of the last item, they were surprisingly sparse.

Aiden began to lead them farther inside the interior. He halted suddenly and held up his hand. When he frantically motioned for them to hide, they rushed to obey, ducking into an old closet. There was a large hole in the wall, allowing Sophie to see out into the room they'd vacated.

A second later she understood why they'd hidden. Two men crashed down the stairs, arms heavy and loaded down. She could see wires sticking out of one of the boxes.

Phillip's men had raided Aiden's base. He was so tense she could see his jaw clenched in the dim closet.

The men departed through a different door than Aiden, Sophie and Celine had entered a few moments earlier. If they had all used the same door... Sophie shivered to realize how close they had come to being discovered.

They waited five minutes, the silence broken only by their breathing. Sophie's breath came in short bursts, her heart thudding in her ears.

When she felt she'd scream if they didn't move, Aiden reached past her and pushed the door open. Without a word, he led them up the stairs into the room on the left. She gasped. When she peered at him, the absolute devastation she saw on his face shocked her.

The room was in shambles. The mattress was shredded. Papers were strewn across the floor. A laptop lay shattered on the floor.

There were wires lying loose. The technology they'd powered was gone.

Sophie had seen some of that technology being carried out of the building.

"We need to go, now!" he ground out. "They'll be expecting me to come back. They won't hesitate to shoot me or anyone with me."

Sophie didn't need to hear more. She grabbed Celine's hand and they ran. When Aiden beat her to the driver's side, she veered to the passenger side with no question. He knew the men they were up against. If they were going to escape with their lives, they needed to move efficiently.

Celine slid into the back seat and Sophie buckled herself in beside Aiden. He was in Reverse and then careening out of the parking lot before her belt had clicked in place.

"How did they know so fast?" Sophie asked after they'd gone five miles. No cars had followed them so far. Hopefully, they had made a clean escape.

"I don't know." His mouth was set in a grim line. "What I do know is every scrap of the evidence I've been collecting for six months is gone. There's still my eyewitness account, but the hard evidence, stuff that would have helped me put Larson away for life, is gone."

All his hard work. All his research and digging— lost. Anything that tied Phillip Larson to Tim's death.

And there was no way to go back. Larson would be cautious now. Aiden knew that he was now on the other man's hit list. Along with the beautiful woman sitting beside him and, no doubt, her little sister. Cute kid. Seemed to have a bit of an attitude. Reminded him of his own kid sister.

The man he'd worked for wanted them both dead. He felt dirty from the association, regardless of the honorable reasons behind his connection.

Aiden curled his lip at the thought of his "boss." Yeah, right. He wanted nothing more than to see the man handcuffed and unable to harm anyone else. Life in prison was exactly what the man deserved, and Aiden prayed he'd get exactly that. More, he prayed that he'd be the one to snap the cuffs in place.

"What are you going to do now?"

He kept his eyes forward. His gut burned with anger. "I don't know. Your uncle is a bad man. He killed my partner, but I'll never be able to prove it now. And there's no possible way for me to go back in and get the hard evidence I need for a conviction. Or even for an arrest."

He turned his head and met Sophie's horrified gaze

before meeting Celine's fascinated one in the mirror. He'd said too much. Certainly more than he'd planned to.

"At least there's no one behind us," he muttered.

"Will they catch up?"

He wouldn't lie to her, no matter how scary the answer was. "They won't stop trying, that you can count on. Until they are behind bars, they'll hunt us down." A high-pitched ding caught his attention. He glanced down at the panel. He'd forgotten about the low-fuel light coming on. Perfect. They were running on fumes. "We gotta stop for gas. Keep an eye out for a station."

Sophie nodded, but didn't say anything. Her face was pale and drawn. She understood the precariousness of their situation. Within a few minutes, they saw signs for a gas station and pulled over.

"Keep low in the car." He turned off the engine. "We don't want anyone to remember seeing you here."

He could see that Celine wanted to argue. Thankfully, she followed her sister's lead. He felt bad for the kid. It wasn't her fault she was messed up in this. Phillip Larson probably knew that Aiden hadn't killed Sophie and Celine. His men would be searching for two red-haired females. Not to mention that Celine's hearing devices—he wasn't sure what they were called—were unique enough to draw unwanted attention. He put the nozzle into the tank and waited, drumming his fingers on the roof of the car. He was tempted to fill up only partially but didn't give in. They needed to go far enough to reach safety, and he had no real idea yet where that safety was.

When the tank reached capacity, he jerked the nozzle

out and replaced it on the pump. A discreet glance into the vehicle confirmed that the sisters were keeping low. He used cash to pay. It wouldn't be good to leave any kind of digital trail. He strode back to the car, deliberately neither talking to Sophie nor looking at either of the sisters until they had pulled out.

"You can sit up now."

Sophie sat up immediately and signed something to her sister. Celine plopped back into her seat with an exaggerated huff. Poor kid. From what he'd heard, he knew that their parents and brother had recently died, leaving the sisters alone.

Matt and Sarah. Those were the names of Sophie's parents. And her brother had been named Brian.

Not for the first time, he wondered if their deaths had been an accident. He knew for a fact that Phillip had not mourned the loss. Oh, he'd been the perfect grieving brother out in public, but in private, Aiden had heard enough to know that Matt had been a problem for Phillip. In fact, Phillip had appeared to take some sort of satisfaction from his brother's passing.

Had Phillip planned his brother's death? It wouldn't be the first death that he'd caused. Phillip Larson was a cold-blooded killer.

Aiden had been ordered to kill Sophie and Celine, hadn't he? But again, there was no physical evidence. Nothing other than his word. Phillip had never actually said to kill them. A skilled defense attorney could argue that his words had been misunderstood.

Now was not the time to worry over it. He needed to get Sophie and her sister to safety. Again he checked the rearview mirror, which he had not adjusted. Reaching up, he gave the mirror a slight tug, moving it only slightly. Come to think of it, he hadn't needed to really adjust the seat, either, which was unusual for him. He was just under six feet. Sophie was fairly tall herself. Maybe five foot nine.

"Where can we go?"

That was a good question. "Let me think."

She was silent while he considered his options.

"I have a good buddy, Levi, a couple hours from here. We were in the military together. I think we can probably stop off at his place for the night."

"You'll stay with us, right?" She bit her lip. "I mean, you won't drop us off and head back to your precinct."

Slightly insulted that she'd think he would abandon them, he scowled at her.

"I wouldn't do that. Even if I were the kind of jerk who'd dump you somewhere, I don't think I can. The fewer people who know that you two are still alive, or your location, the better. As I said earlier, we don't know who or where the information leak is coming from."

He let the words settle between them.

He needed to be ready. Later, he'd risk one more call in to his chief. Hopefully, he'd be able to make it to Levi's house before Phillip's men caught up to them. He needed to cut his hair. Change his appearance so that he wouldn't be recognized on sight. He knew how to blend in. That was one thing that had made him ideal for undercover work. As a kid, he'd lived in a dysfunctional family where standing out often led to an unpleasant, frequently painful situation. He'd learned well the art of going unnoticed. Now he used those skills and the features God had given him to do his job. Brown hair, brown eyes, no noteworthy tattoos or scars that people would recall later.

At least no scars on the outside. He kicked the thought out as soon as it entered his mind.

If only the women he was with would blend in, as well. He sent a sidelong look at Sophie. She was tall, and she had fiery red hair grazing her shoulders without a hint of curl. She was worth a second look. Or a third. Celine had the same red hair and the same fair complexion. Nope, the two girls would stand out in a crowd. Plus, Celine's hearing devices. He had no idea how much she could hear without them. As visible as they were, he believed asking her to not wear them would be putting them more at risk. If she took them off, he was pretty sure that she'd need to rely on sign language. It was a gorgeous sight, he admitted to himself, watching the sisters converse silently, but it was conspicuous. They couldn't afford that. He turned to merge onto the toll road.

There was nothing he could do about it. He drove up to the tollbooth.

He grabbed a ticket at the tollbooth and headed east.

It was almost an hour later when he realized they were in trouble.

"Get down," he ordered Sophie.

She signed something to her sister. The girl gasped and ducked down. Sophie slid lower as much as she could.

"Aiden?"

He checked the rearview mirror. His hands tightened reflexively on the wheel. Experimentally, he sped up. The car behind them also increased speed.

The buffer he'd hoped to put between them and Phillip's men was gone.

"We're being followed."

The blood drained from Sophie's already pale face.

Were these the same men from his base? Or had Phillip called in more of his people for an all-out search? The pit dropped out of his stomach. He ignored it. Reflexively, his left hand slid down to his side to touch the revolver strapped there. He was armed, but probably not enough to withstand an assault from multiple attackers. If his vehicle was disabled and they needed to go on foot, they would be at a definite disadvantage.

He glanced into the mirror again. The car was still on his tail. Another one joined it.

They needed a way out—fast.

FOUR

Aiden pushed the gas pedal down as far as it would go. The sedan shot forward. A glance in the mirror was all it took to prove that, yes, they were in fact being followed. The van tailing them sped up, keeping pace with them. When he switched lanes, it followed suit, cutting off other cars without hesitation. The second vehicle remained in the other lane, moving faster now. It was going to cut them off.

Aiden clenched his teeth. They were traveling at the maximum speed.

This was not a good situation.

"How did they know?" Sophie said, her voice a tight whisper. "How did they find where we were going?"

He shrugged, but tension was gnawing away at him. He needed to keep these two women safe. That was all that mattered now. But the question of how they were found so fast wouldn't leave him alone. "It must be your car. Phillip must have known what you drive. He would have seen me leave in your vehicle. I arrived on a motorcycle."

"Now what?"

"Now? We have to find a way to lose them. I can't do anything while they're after us. I definitely can't take you to my buddy's house. Not with a tail."

"How do you plan on doing that? Losing them, I mean."

He'd known what she meant. He just wasn't sure he knew the answer to her question.

He decided now was the perfect time to ask for a little divine intervention. They wouldn't be getting out of this on their own power, that was for sure. It would be awesome if God listened this time. He shoved away the unworthy thought. It had been tough holding on to his faith after Tim had died in an ambush, leaving behind a widow and a small son. He had clung to God, though, trusting Him to bring him out of the danger and darkness intact.

He uttered a quick prayer. Sophie shifted beside him. He might have made her uncomfortable with his prayer, but they had more urgent matters than comfort.

"I don't have a plan, not yet." He chanced another glance in the mirror. Unbelievable. Who knew vans were that fast? "Right now, I'm open to suggestions."

"First thing I suggest is that we get off the toll road," she responded, taking him at his word. "Otherwise, we're bound to hit traffic soon."

She was right. They were bound to hit either construction or traffic from people going into the city. He needed to get off this road, and soon.

"I hope you don't have any outstanding traffic tickets," he remarked.

She tossed him a quizzical glance. "No. Why?"

He veered and headed for the exit, cutting off the second car. It was close. The driver hadn't been expecting the move and jerked to the side. He jerked too hard and spun into the guardrail and then continued on past the upcoming exit. "You're going to get one for not paying your toll."

The sedan sailed down the exit ramp and through the E-Z Pass lane. He smirked when he saw that the van had come to a stop when a couple of tractor-trailer rigs boxed it in.

His smugness faded. They didn't have a lot of time. Traffic wouldn't hold their pursuers for long. And Larson now knew with absolute certainty which vehicle Aiden and the sisters were driving. They had to find a new car. Fast.

Celine sat up in the back seat. She signed something to Sophie.

"What is she saying?" he said. He was somewhat worried that she was signing and not using her voice. "Is she okay?"

"She's scared."

He knew the feeling.

The van hadn't caught up to them yet. Up ahead was the turnoff to go to Levi's house. Did he dare risk it?

Did he really have a choice? They couldn't stay in the sedan that Sophie owned. They were a moving target in it. He knew that Phillip Larson had people on his payroll in at least three states. That was a lot of power to round up searchers. There were no other options. Decision made, he swung onto the back road, heading in the direction of the farm, the back end of the car swinging wide on the loose rocks. Sophie's arm shot out as she braced herself against the dashboard.

"Sorry," he muttered, even though he'd do the same thing again if the situation arose. Her safety, and the safety of the girl in the back seat, came before all other considerations. Thankfully, the weather was holding out. At least for now. The temperature had started to dip into the fifties, and he could see dark clouds invading the skyline, blocking out the sunlight.

Storms were headed this way. In more ways than one.

There were too many ruts and potholes in the road to miss. He wished he could slow down but didn't dare. The uneven surface under the tires made the whole vehicle vibrate. He unclenched his jaw and flexed his shoulders, feeling some of the tension drain away. He relaxed slightly, knowing that they were no longer on the main road. Levi had always valued his privacy. Hence the house in a field in the middle of the country.

His cell phone vibrated. He looked at the screen. It was the chief again. He put it on speaker so he had use of both hands. "Hey, Chief, I have you on speaker."

That was code for *civilians can listen in.*

"Right. Where are you now, Aiden? We have reports of a lot of movement at the Larson residence."

Phillip was mobilizing.

"I'm off to see a friend to talk about transportation."

She processed that. "Okay. I want you to keep a low profile for a day or so. I can't go into specifics, but there has been intel that you are in a dangerous place."

"I already know that, ma'am. Two vehicles were tailing us a few miles back. Lost them, but I don't know for how long."

"Understood. Check in every four hours or so, and let me know your status. Use my cell phone number and try to avoid contacting anyone else for the time being. The fewer people in the loop on this one, the more secure you'll be."

And the safer the Larson girls would be. He heard what she didn't say. They were closing in on the breach and whoever had access to his data.

"As you wish. We'll keep our heads down."

He disconnected. For a moment he said nothing.

"What does she mean about you being in a dangerous place?" Sophie asked.

He wasn't surprised that she had caught on. "It means that she has a good idea where the leak is coming from and that it's from a source that leaves us all vulnerable."

"So where can we hide that we won't be found while they fix the situation?"

"I have no idea."

He was a man who liked to be in control. But he had absolutely no control over this whole case anymore. His cover was blown. He had no backup. And he was the only person standing between the sisters and those who would kill them. Whatever actions he took could literally mean life or death for them.

Shifting his eyes to Sophie's, he saw something in her bright gaze that he hadn't anticipated. Trust. Despite all she'd been through, this woman had chosen to put her trust and her faith in him.

And that terrified him more than anything else.

* * *

Aiden had gone to a dark place in his mind. Sophie could see the wall he had put between them. She had no idea what was going on in his head; however, she believed God would protect them. For whatever reason, He had chosen to work through this man. She would trust, although it wasn't easy. In pursuit of her career, she'd allowed herself to drift away from God. Something that never should have happened.

She peered at the shuttered expression of the man beside her. His prayer had surprised her, and if she was honest, it had made her uncomfortable. Prayer, she was ashamed to admit, had not been her instinctive response. She knew there was something dark in Aiden's past; she could see the brokenness in him. Could sense it in the way he held himself aloof that he had wounds from the past that hadn't yet healed.

Didn't they all?

It had been a little under a month since the death of her parents and brother had shattered her world. In that short period of time, she'd gone from a single woman with a promising career as a commercial designer to a stand-in single parent for her devastated sibling. She'd taken time off her job on family leave to get Celine settled. It was the right thing to do, but the change had completely shifted her world and her priorities.

And now she was on the run from a man who wanted her dead. A man who was her own flesh and blood. It was difficult to wrap her head around.

Was she crazy to trust a total stranger when her own family was failing her? Possibly. She felt safe with

Aiden in a way she couldn't remember feeling in such a long time. She wished she could give him some comfort in some way. Her fingers twitched, longing to reach out and touch his arm in solidarity.

He'd think she was crazy.

Ruthlessly, she squashed the foolish urge. What had come over her? She was not one to get touchy-feely, never had been. Even hugging her family made her slightly uncomfortable.

She'd never be able to hug anyone in her family except Celine ever again.

Her eyes burned and she blinked back the sudden wetness.

"You okay?"

She wasn't surprised that Aiden had noticed her sudden distress. Very little seemed to escape his notice. She was touched, and also wary. She shook her head.

"I'm good." She changed the subject. "So, tell me more about this friend of yours."

She shifted in her seat so that she could watch him better.

"As I mentioned before, I have a buddy from my days in the military. He's gone off the grid, likes to keep to himself. But I know that he has a home in the middle of nowhere out here. I have no idea if he's home, but he should be okay with us dropping by."

That sounded like a good plan. Still, her stomach tightened up. She didn't know this military buddy of his. And he didn't seem to know much about what the guy was up to these days, although maybe he was just being stingy with the details.

Still.

She'd feel a whole lot better once she could assess whether they were truly safe with him. It was controlling of her, a part of herself she recognized, but her baby sister's life was at stake. Cecile was the only one Sophie had left, and vice versa. She didn't want to take unnecessary risks at this point.

"Are you positive we can trust him?" She didn't want to insult him, but how well did he know this guy?

Aiden shrugged. "Well enough. You don't go through war together and not develop a bond. Levi's saved my life a time or two, and I've returned the favor."

He stopped talking, and she knew that he'd locked the door on his private past. She wouldn't be getting any more personal information from him. At least, not on this topic.

He made another turn onto a narrow gravel road.

Sighing, she turned to stare out the window. Each minute took them farther away from the populated towns. The distance between houses widened. The landscape she saw was covered with lush trees, grass and spring flora. As she watched, a doe grazing near the side of the road perked up her ears and raised her white tail. She sprang back into the trees on her long, graceful legs. Two spotted fawns followed close behind. She watched, fascinated. There weren't many deer where she had lived for the past few years.

Aiden slowed.

"What are you doing?" Why would he slow when they were in danger?

He flashed an unexpected grin her way. Her pulse jumped.

"I'm waiting to see if she—" he nodded in the direction of the deer "—has any more friends."

"Friends…" She snapped her mouth shut as another deer bounded across the road and dashed into the trees.

"There she is. They are rarely alone. And they don't seem to recognize that running in front of cars is more dangerous than staying put."

He resumed his previous speed. Less than an hour later, they slowed again. This time, Aiden turned onto a lane. Really, it was little more than a tractor path winding between a dense row of trees. Glancing up, she saw what appeared to be a small speaker hooked to a tree. She might have missed it, its color almost exactly matching the bark of the tree. Arching her neck, she looked around. It wasn't the only one. She could see that several of the trees appeared to have similar devices attached to them.

Celine moved closer to the window to peer out. They moved silently down the path. It was so long that Sophie was ready to ask Aiden if he was sure they were going the correct route when the path suddenly opened up and she could view fields and a large barn. And cows. More cows than she had seen in her life.

"Oh, look at that cute house!" Celine blurted out.

It was straight out of a storybook. A little blue farmhouse. She blinked.

"I thought farms were supposed to have large houses," she murmured. "That's the smallest farmhouse I have ever seen."

Aiden grinned, anticipation glowing on his face. "Isn't it great? We built it, Levi and I."

"You built it?"

She couldn't help being impressed. No one in her family had ever built anything.

"Yep. After we got back from Afghanistan. Levi wanted his own place, something simple. He had inherited land that was vacant. We got a crew together, designed it and built it." He lifted his eyes to meet Celine's in the mirror. "Just don't tell him his house is cute."

She grinned at him and sat back.

Sophie raised her eyebrows.

"It's not cute," he insisted. "It's a very rugged structure."

She laughed and caught his gaze. Something electrical passed between them.

The pride was there in his eyes. And something more. A longing that had her own throat closing. She knew what it was like to want something you couldn't have. What was it that he wanted?

"Sophie, can I borrow your phone for a minute? I want to let my chief know that we've found a place."

She frowned. "What if your leak or mole is watching and sees the number?"

"That's why we're using your phone and why I'm calling my chief's private phone. She has a phone with a number that only a few of us know."

She handed him her phone, still wary. He took it and dialed quickly. "Hey, Chief. Yeah, we're good. I'm not going to give you the details, but we're hoping to find shelter off the grid for a few days at an old buddy's place."

She listened carefully. Aiden ended the call and she realized he hadn't said where they were, or even named his buddy. Her tightened muscles loosened.

They tightened again when the front door opened. A man walked out of the house, suspicion shining through the scowl that scrunched up his face. Aiden continued to drive forward slowly. Sophie's stomach cramped with anxiety. This man did not appear friendly. No, sir. He glared at the car. His legs were braced and his back straight, ready for an attack. She could see the soldier in his stance. His dark eyes were cold as he looked at her through the car window. Maybe this wasn't such a good idea. She opened her mouth to tell Aiden they should leave, but it was too late. He had stopped the car and switched off the ignition. Pocketing the keys, he opened the door and started to get out.

"I'm scared," Celine whispered, her eyes huge as she took in the soldier.

Aiden halted and pivoted slightly. Bending, he reached in, tapped the girl's shoulder and waited until she dragged her attention back to him.

"Celine, it will be okay. I promise, no matter what happens, I will protect you and your sister. Okay?"

As he addressed Celine, there was a softness in his eyes that hadn't been there before. His voice was velvet and steel. He meant what he said. He would protect them at all costs. A chunk of the ice that had formed around her heart since the death of her parents and

Brian melted. She hadn't even known how much she wanted assurance that he would see this through until he spoke. They needed a protector.

Shame bristled inside. She hadn't turned to God when the trouble started. Had she grown so focused on her career that her instincts to run to her Father had faded?

Celine nodded at Aiden, and he resumed his mission to greet his former comrade.

The soldier still didn't appear too welcoming.

As he stepped off the porch, she could see that his right arm was actually a prosthetic limb. Here was a soldier who had lost something in battle.

The two men stared at each other for three seconds, and then Levi's face broke open into a wide grin. The joy in that smile was incredible.

"Aiden! I was beginning to think you'd forgotten me."

"Not so. I was on a job. Deep cover." The two men shook hands and slapped shoulders. "I need your help."

Levi nodded his head. "Of course, of course. Whatever you need." A line appeared in his forehead as he tilted his head. "Are you in trouble, say?"

Sophie blinked. She had never heard anyone phrase a question just that way before. Not only that. There was something different about the way Levi talked. He had a subtle accent that she couldn't quite place.

Aiden glanced around, the frown on his face becoming more pronounced. "I think this is a discussion that we would be better off having inside. It would be safer for everyone."

Levi's eyes flared wide. Whatever he expected his old friend to say, it apparently wasn't that. To his credit, he didn't argue. Instead, he stepped back and swung the door open with his uninjured arm.

"*Ja*, come in."

Sophie felt her jaw drop open. She quickly closed her mouth, hoping that nobody had noticed. Now that she heard him speak some more, she realized why Levi's voice sounded so different. The young man in front of them was Amish. She had never heard of an Amish man fighting in the military. Her minimal experience and knowledge indicated that the Amish were pacifists and would not fight even to protect themselves. But not only had this man fought in a war, he had lost his arm in combat.

Obviously, there was a story here. Well, whatever the man's background was, she said a silent prayer that he would be able to help them. Their options were growing slimmer by the moment.

Her uncle was persistent—he would not give up until he found them. It was up to the two men now talking quietly in the middle of the room to protect them all.

FIVE

Sophie let the door swing closed behind her and Celine. Aiden was already moving through the room, peering out of the windows and pulling the blinds closed. Levi, she noted, caught what was going on and strode to the kitchen area, copying Aiden's actions. Amish or not, this young man seemed to be aware that danger was lurking.

He wasn't dressed Amish. Instead of the typical bowl-cut hairstyle, his sandy blond hair was cut short, only about an inch long all over his head. His one ear sported a small gold earring, and if she wasn't mistaken, he had a tattoo peeking out from underneath the collar of his T-shirt. No, definitely not very Amish in appearance. But his voice and inflections still made her wonder.

Aiden completed his task and rejoined her in the center of the room. He kept silent until his friend joined him.

"As I was saying, we could use your assistance." His voice was low, a deep rumble. She glanced at Celine, whose eyes were glued to his face, intense. She had not been able to hear his words. They were too low for her to catch them even with her cochlears on.

"Anything," Levi responded immediately. "You know that. Whatever I have is yours."

Some of the tension drained out of Aiden's posture. He rubbed the back of his neck, turning his head as if to stretch the muscles. She could relate. Her head was beginning to ache from all the stress.

"Thanks. We need a vehicle. It's a long story, and though I don't think I can tell you everything because of the confidential nature of some of it, I will tell you what I can."

"Oh?" Levi slid a glance to Sophie and then back to Aiden. He raised his eyebrows. There seemed to be some hidden meaning behind the query.

"Not what you think. I'm protecting them."

What exactly did Levi think? Whatever it was, she was sure that the tips of Aiden's ears were red.

"So this isn't Janet?"

Aiden growled. "No. That's over."

The smile faded from Levi's face. "*Ach*. Sorry, man. Didn't mean to interfere."

What would he be interfering with? Sophie tucked the questions away. Now wasn't the time to ask him personal questions, although she was curious to know about this Janet. Obviously, the woman was someone who had meant something to him.

She wasn't jealous. Of course not. That would be ridiculous. The man was helping them escape from their own uncle. She flinched away from dwelling too deeply on the fact that her father's brother could have such evil intentions. Aiden was speaking, and she needed to pay attention.

"Don't worry about it. She and I are history. It's for the best. Anyway, can you help?"

"*Ja*, absolutely. Whatever you want. There's a truck in the garage. Or I have an old car I've been repairing. It's old, but it will get you where you want to go. The tire treads are worn down, but not too bad."

Aiden scratched his chin as he pondered their choices. "The car. Less conspicuous."

"The car it is. Why don't y'all come into the kitchen and get something to eat while I clean the car out."

She waited until Aiden motioned for them to join him. Celine stepped close to her side. So close she could feel her sister's slim body trembling. The preteen tried to keep an indifferent expression on her face, but Sophie could see the way her teeth were bruising her bottom lip from her fear and anxiety. Trepidation shivered in the air. The poor kid didn't know who to trust anymore.

As discreetly as she could, Sophie nudged her sister. Startled, Celine jerked her head toward her.

"I'll be right here. I won't leave you, and I will protect you," Sophie signed.

"Promise?" Celine signed back.

"Promise."

"Okay." Celine reverted back to using her voice. The sisters followed the men into the kitchen. It was surprisingly light and airy. The walls were a bright, cheerful yellow and the counters were trendy—frosty quartz with a black-and-white-marbled effect. There were no other frills or decor in the room, which might have been because he was a guy, or it may have been due to his possible Amish heritage.

Aiden was not walking comfortable in the house. He moved to the window and moved the blind slightly to scan outside, his jaw tight and hands clenched.

"Aiden, I have plenty of food in the refrigerator," Levi offered. "You can help yourself to whatever you need."

He glanced once more out the window before letting the blind fall back into place and turning away. He didn't look happy. Seeing him so tense was making her feel antsy. She half expected her uncle or one of his henchmen to come busting through the front door at any moment.

"Relax, my friend. I have an alarm system installed. If anyone turns down my lane, I will know about it. It's *gut*, ain't so?"

Now she was convinced. Levi might not be Amish anymore, but somewhere in the past, he had been. She would never ask about it. One didn't grow up in Pennsylvania without knowing that leaving an Amish community was never something done lightly. And it was deeply personal.

Didn't mean she wasn't curious, though.

Celine looked a bit puzzled. If Sophie had to guess, she'd say that her sister hadn't understood what their host had said.

"He said there's an alarm system, so we will know if anyone approaches the house," she told her sister, signing to make sure she understood. Celine's wrinkled brow smoothed out.

"It's true." Levi nodded and gestured to the front of the house with his prosthetic arm. "I like my privacy."

Aiden slapped him lightly on the shoulder. "I remember that. I really appreciate your help. We were in a bind, that's for sure."

His friend shrugged.

Levi didn't appear phased by the fact that Celine was deaf, nor did she react to the fact that he had a prosthesis. He welcomed them into his home. Aiden set about finding them something to eat. Their meal consisted of cold-cut sandwiches, bananas, store-bought potato salad and milk. She was so hungry it all tasted delicious.

Celine ate like she'd not eaten for a week. Sophie smiled to herself. When Aiden raised an eyebrow at her, she merely shrugged. She couldn't tell him that only yesterday, when Sophie had made Celine grilled cheese for lunch, she had complained that sandwiches were boring and for children.

Taking a bite of her own ham, cheese and pickle sandwich, she held in a groan of pleasure when the flavors hit her tongue. She hadn't been hungry, not really, since her parents and brother had died. Suddenly ravenous, she focused all her attention on her meal. The sounds of conversation died and were replaced with the gentle scrapes of glassware on the table and silverware scratching the bottoms of the plates as the hungry group devoured the potato salad and sandwiches.

Sophie finished her meal and reached for her water glass. A loud, high-pitched alarm sounded three times. She knocked the glass over. Water streamed down the length of the table and dribbled off the opposite edge.

Aiden leaped to his feet, pulling his service weapon from its harness in one smooth motion. He shifted his stance and ran to the window. He stood to the left side, his back against the wall and his weapon held up as he peered out the window, his dark eyes searching the yard. Levi had also gotten to his feet. Instead of going to the window, though, his eyes were glued to a small screen.

He had cameras aimed at the driveway.

Celine didn't react to the alarm. It was too high for her to hear. She did, however, react to the men jumping up. Her eyes filled with tears and her complexion paled so much Sophie thought she'd pass out.

"I don't see anyone," Aiden called to Levi.

"I do," Levi responded, his voice flat. Their host had reverted back to a soldier. Aiden left his post at the window and raced to Levi's side.

He pointed to the screen. A vehicle was moving at a snail's pace down the lane. Probably hoping to avoid being heard. "That's definitely Phillip's man."

Sophie met Aiden's flat stare. How had they found them so quickly?

"They're driving really slow," Sophie murmured, placing her arm around Celine's shaking form. Her sister didn't resist. She was truly terrified.

"That's good news," Aiden announced. "That gives us some time to maneuver."

He raised an eyebrow at Levi in a signal the other man appeared to understand.

"That's so. It would be best if you take the truck. Follow me."

Levi turned and slipped out the back door.

Aiden gestured for the two women to precede him. As they moved past him, he placed a hand on each one's shoulder.

"I meant what I said. I'll get you out of this. No matter what. Just do exactly as I tell you."

Levi led the silent group out toward the garage, gesturing for them to stick to the shadows of the trees that lined the property. Once they reached the garage, instead of going inside the weathered building, they continued along the outside wall.

A low rumble and the sound of gravel crunching under wheels reached Aiden's ears. Levi turned his head and nodded.

The van was creeping closer to the house. Aiden glanced back, still not seeing it. But if he could hear it, it was only a matter of seconds.

"We need to hurry."

"*Ja*. Keep low," Levi said, gesturing with his hand and imitating the posture. For Celine's sake, no doubt.

Sophie nodded and reached back to grab her sister's hand. Celine was still pale, but she was making a brave effort to do everything that the adults did. The kid was impressing him with her grit. This was not a situation any twelve-year-old should have to deal with, ever, and yet she hadn't complained at all. At least not that he had heard. If she had signed any complaints to Sophie, he'd missed them.

He was reminded of his own sweet baby sister, Jennie. She'd been about Celine's age when they'd landed in foster care and been separated. The thought of his sister was a sharp knife to his heart. He'd tried to connect with her after they'd both aged out of the system, but she had shut him out.

He'd failed her.

Well, he wouldn't fail Celine or her beautiful older sister, either.

And why he was thinking of Sophie that way when they were in a crisis situation was beyond him. He needed to get his head back where it belonged. Which meant he needed to not notice how lovely or strong or brave Sophie Larson was. Because, no matter how wonderful she was, it was her uncle that was after them. He couldn't forget that if she hadn't shown up early, his cover would not have been blown.

Or would it have?

The swiftness with which Phillip acted made him wonder if he had already been found out. It was entirely possible that if Sophie and her sister hadn't shown up, he'd have been ambushed at his base. Then he'd be dead. At least now they had a chance.

The small group continued past the garage, keeping low as Levi had instructed. Beyond that, there was a barn. They skirted an old, untethered Amish buggy before entering the barn. The buggy was black and shaped like a large box. The front window was intact although the side one was broken out. Aiden could see that the wheel on the far side was bent at an awkward angle.

Levi must do repairs for some of the local Amish communities. Aiden had never asked if Levi's own family lived nearby. He figured if his friend wanted to discuss his past, he would. So far, he hadn't. That was fine. He hadn't told Levi about Jennie, either.

Only Janet, his fiancée. Ex-fiancée. She couldn't take the life he led.

Cops didn't make good husbands, as far as he could figure.

"Where are they?" he muttered, glancing over his shoulder. They should have seen them by now.

A screen door slammed.

"In the house," Levi answered. A sudden loud crash inside the house made the man wince.

"Aw, sorry, man."

"Stuff." The soldier shrugged. "It's only stuff. All the important things are here."

True. He moved closer to Sophie, the urge to keep close and protect her and Celine racing in his veins. They were so close that, as she moved, her red hair tickled his arm. It was soft. He inhaled deeply. Her hair smelled like strawberries. It fit. Fresh and vibrant.

Slam!

Startled, Aiden pivoted on his heel. The back door of the house had been flung open and the men were raging outside, their boots thudding down the stairs. Both had rifles. They needed to move. Now.

"Run!" he shouted, placing a hand on Sophie's back and another on Celine's. The small group ceased trying to be inconspicuous and took off, Levi in the lead. He heard a shot, but it missed them. A gun barked a second time. *Thunk.* This time, the shooter had hit something. Aiden thought it was the buggy. Well, better a buggy or a car than one of them.

Levi jumped into the truck and they piled in after him, Sophie and Celine sitting in the back. When Levi turned the key and the engine turned over but didn't start, Aiden started praying. Sweat broke out on his forehead as Levi turned the key again and the motor revved and sputtered. A hand grabbed on to Aiden's shoulder and held tight.

Sophie. She was leaning against the seat, eyes so wide they were ready to pop out of their sockets. He could tell by the angle of her other arm that she was holding on to Celine.

Instinctively, he reached up and grabbed her hand to give her silent comfort. She turned her hand over and squeezed his.

Another gunshot. Closer. The back fender pinged.

Too close.

With a final rev, the engine erupted to life, choking and gurgling like it was on death's door. Levi threw the vehicle into Reverse and the truck shot backward, bouncing as it hit ruts in the yard. Without fully stopping, he shoved it into Drive and they were off. Aiden threw out an arm to brace himself, feeling the bump as Sophie hit the back of his seat.

A fourth shot hit the back window. Celine and Sophie screamed.

He winced and cast his gaze to the side mirror. The two men who'd been shooting at them were running back to their van.

"This is going to be a short trip," Levi muttered. "I think they hit the gas tank."

Aiden locked eyes with Levi, then looked down

to the gas gauge. It was slowly decreasing even as he watched. He bit off a groan. What now?

"Where would be the safest place around here to ditch the truck?"

Sophie gasped in the back but didn't say anything.

He was still holding her hand. It felt natural, their hands clasped together, and he liked it. Big mistake. He forced himself to let go of her hand, which slid off his shoulder. He wanted to look at her and at the same time didn't want to risk it. The connection he was feeling to this woman was happening at the worst possible time. It was stealing his focus, and he couldn't allow that to continue.

His hand felt empty.

"Well, now, I have a friend around here who might help. I've been helping him get several cars ready for crash-up derbies this summer, so he might be inclined to help."

"Why?" Sophie's soft voice floated up from the back seat. She was still leaning forward. Her breath whispered against his ear.

Levi flashed a hurried grin in the rearview mirror. "I didn't charge him. He owes me."

Without warning, the soldier spun the truck off the road and into a field at the side of the road. They could barely see out the windows, the grass was so high. He kept going at a fast clip.

Aiden loved driving fast, but driving with Levi was an adventure he didn't always enjoy.

"Buddy, shouldn't you slow down?"

"I can see fine enough. And we need to be fast, ain't

so?" he said as the truck hit an especially ferocious rut. Aiden's head nearly hit the roof. Still, they sped on.

"I do love four-wheel drive," the former Amish man sang out.

Celine giggled in the back seat. Aiden caught Sophie's gaze. She smiled—the first real smile he'd seen all day. Great. He was riding with a bunch of thrill seekers.

Then she looked at her sister and he knew it wasn't the thrill she smiled at, but her sister's joy. He remembered that their parents and brother were dead. How often did the kid laugh?

Not much, most likely.

Soon, though not soon enough, Levi halted the truck. "We'd best leave this here. No one will see it from the road, *ja*?"

Aiden nodded. "Yeah, we can hoof it from here."

As they filed out of the truck, Aiden pondered their situation.

How had Phillip's men located them so fast? He had lost them, he knew he had. When he had a moment, he'd check Sophie's phone to make sure there wasn't a tracking device or a bug in it.

A tracking device. Of course. How could he have been so stupid! The leak was within or close to the police department. Obviously, anyone with close ties to the department would have the ability to use the GPS on his phone to find his location.

They needed to dump their phones. All of them. Otherwise, they would be found no matter where they went.

"Wait. Sophie. Let's leave our cell phones here. Just in case someone is tracking them."

"Hold on." Levi pulled out his phone and dialed. Sophie looked at Aiden, her face full of questions. He heard Levi telling the person on the other end that some-one had broken into his house.

"Levi," Aiden muttered. "What are you thinking?"

"Hey, I told them that I wasn't home. You heard that? For all they know, I got an alert that my alarm went off. They'll send someone over to check for those guys, and maybe they'll catch them. If anyone saw them leaving, they might be caught and we could relax a bit."

"I wish we'd discussed this first."

Sophie got his attention. "So do you still want us to leave our phones here?"

"Yeah."

If they found the phones here, they'd be in the mid-dle of a cornfield. Literally. No clue to where they were headed next.

Sophie hadn't liked the idea, he could tell. To his relief, she surrendered her phone. Then she looked at her sister.

Celine's face was filled with teenage horror. "Leave my phone? It has all my contacts on it!"

Aiden bit back a chuckle. It wasn't funny, but she re-minded him of Jennie more and more. Sweet and sassy. He'd bet she was capable of some pretty fierce angst.

Well, he couldn't do anything for Jennie—she wouldn't let him—but he could be there for Celine. He placed his hands on her shoulders. "Celine, we can get you a new phone. Right now, those devices are putting all of us, including Levi, in danger. We have no choice."

The struggle was mirrored on her face for three seconds before she yanked the offending device out of her back pocket and threw it down in the grass.

"There. Happy?"

"No. But I will be when y'all are safe."

For the briefest second, a soft smile flickered before it was replaced with a nonchalant expression.

"Whatever."

Sophie rolled her eyes, then smiled at him. Electricity sizzled in the air between them. He pulled his gaze back before he got lost in it. But he still felt it. He needed to create some distance between them. As he walked past her, she reached out and squeezed his hand in silent thanks. He squeezed back before dropping his phone and starting off again.

A new concern popped into his head. He had literally led these killers right to Levi's door. Not only were Sophie, Celine and himself in danger, but now Levi was, as well, just by association.

"Levi, what will you do? I don't know if you can go back to your house now."

Guilt smacked him right in the face. And weren't they now risking his neighbor, too? "Maybe we shouldn't go to your neighbor."

"Naw. It's *gut*. You guys can make some phone calls. We'll think of a plan."

Aiden nodded, but his stomach clenched. A plan that included hiding a tall, beautiful redhead who would stick out anywhere and her sweet, very cute deaf sister. Without phones. And without being able to rely on his chief and fellow officers for backup.

The situation seemed to grow more hopeless by the minute.

SIX

She wished she could take his hand again. It was an absurd thought. She didn't even know Aiden. Only hours ago, she had been sure he was going to kill her and Celine.

It was foolish thinking. She clenched her hands together.

When he'd held her hand after she'd unthinkingly grabbed his shoulder back in the truck, it had grounded her in a way she couldn't explain. The anxiety building up inside her had ebbed enough to allow her to draw in a full breath. She felt she'd been barely breathing since the moment her uncle had found her in his home. Aiden's strong grip had made her feel protected. More than that, she'd felt cherished in a way she'd not felt since before she'd left home.

But she was not going to grab his hand again. She had done it to say thanks when he'd talked Celine down from her outrage. That was more than she should have done. She would not encourage the attraction that was springing up between the two of them. Oh, she was aware that he was feeling something, too.

She'd seen the way his eyes had darkened when he'd looked at her.

She had also noticed that he had moved away like he'd been struck by lightning.

Yeah, he felt it. And he didn't want it.

Well, neither did she. She'd ignored her sister to build her career for the past four years. She graduated from college and moved to Chicago without looking back. Her parents had been happy for her, and Brian had called her often. He'd even driven down to visit five or six times after he got his driver's license. But Celine? She'd been away at the school for the deaf during the week and her parents wanted her at home on the weekends. And Sophie had been too busy to find the time to use the videophone and talk with her sister more than a couple of times a year. That was done. She had the chance to reconnect with her sibling and prove to her that she wouldn't abandon her.

A man was not part of her plan.

They'd been walking for at least ten minutes before Aiden spoke again.

"It's safe. Let's cross here. Levi says we'll go around to the back of the house and knock on the door."

Aiden's whisper broke into her contemplation. She nodded to show she understood and signed the instructions to her sister. Once they were all aware of the plan, they ran across the dirt road.

Levi's friend lived in a large yellow farmhouse that desperately needed someone to slap a fresh coat of paint on it. Not to mention the front gutters were in need of repair. Somewhere inside the house, a dog barked.

When the dog continued to bark, she frowned. What if no one was home?

"Aiden."

He turned at her whisper.

"What if it was your actual phone call that told them where we were?" she asked, thinking out loud. "What if someone has your chief's phones all tagged or bugged, or whatever? Even her private line."

He smiled briefly at her wording before falling serious again. That smile tangled up her emotions and kicked her heart into overdrive. She kept her expression bland. There was nothing to do about the heat flaring in her cheeks.

He raised an eyebrow at her blush but didn't comment on it.

"I thought about that. It's possible, but I doubt it. Very few people know where Levi lives. He's been off the grid for a while now. I think it would have taken longer to find us. No, I think it's more likely that they used the GPS on our phones. But I won't call her from Levi's friend's house. We'll pick up a burner phone, something that is hard to trace and I can dump after using, if necessary. But we do need a place to plan. And it's going to storm, so getting out of the weather for the night wouldn't hurt."

She cast a glance at the clouds forming overhead. She hadn't even noticed the sunlight dimming. It was growing later, too. Soon they would be walking in the dark if they continued.

Her legs shook with exhaustion and fear as they climbed the steps to the back porch. The screen was shut but the main door was wide open. A television set was blaring somewhere inside. Someone was home. Her momentary relief was dwarfed by a new worry. What if this friend refused to help? Or what if he thought they were lying and called the police?

"Breathe, Sophie." Aiden leaned in close, his breath fanning her face. She smelled mint. "I'm here, and I will protect you. I promise."

The warmth of his strong hand on her shoulder steadied her enough to smile and nod in response. "I'm okay. Just a little nervous."

His hand pressed down and then was gone.

She could do this.

Levi pounded on the door. Obviously, he had no intention of being subtle. She tugged on Celine's hair affectionately when the girl snuggled up against her side. Then she blushed. Without realizing it, she had done the same thing to Aiden, pressing up against his left side, her hand gripping his forearm. Mortified, she shifted to create space between them.

He gifted her with a lopsided half smile. Her face was on fire. She stared ahead and waited to see who answered the door.

No one answered.

"Is he home, you think?" Aiden mused.

"*Ja*, he's home. He wouldn't leave the door wide open if he had left."

Levi pounded again. "Brad! Ya in there?"

A loud yawn answered, followed by the creak of a piece of furniture. Leaning over slightly, Sophie saw a man of medium height rising from the couch he'd been on. She felt guilty, but still she silently urged him to hurry. Standing out in the open like this was like they were all easy targets. She could practically feel the bull's-eye on her back.

"Hold on. Where's the fire?" Brad muttered as he shuffled to the door, yawning again. "Levi? What's going on?"

"I'll explain in a moment. Can we come in?"

Brad shrugged and motioned for them to enter. A handsome yellow Labrador next to him growled and barked at them even as her tail wagged. Sophie kept her distance. She didn't trust big dogs.

"Easy, Peaches. You know Levi." The dog walked over to the small group. She especially seemed to take to Celine, who immediately crouched down and hugged the animal, burying her face in the canine's furry neck. Peaches's tail thumped on the ground in doggy joy.

"Sorry to intrude on you, Brad. I didn't mean to wake you up."

"It's all right. I was out late on a fire call. Didn't get to bed until four this morning. I must have dozed off while watching the news."

A furious high-pitched beeping interrupted them.

"Hold on." Brad held up one hand. "That's my department."

A dispatcher's voice filled the room. There was some static, so Sophie missed the first part of what the woman said. Brad scrunched his brow and tilted his head, listening.

"…shots fired at 33491 Pless Road, the Burkholder residence…"

His brows rose and he stepped back, glancing at Levi in alarm.

"Are you in trouble, Levi?"

Sophie could hear the hidden question in his words. Are these folks dangerous? His gaze grew less concerned as he took in Celine, still hugging his dog. Who could look at the petite twelve-year-old and think she was dangerous? And she certainly didn't look like she was scared to be with Sophie and Aiden, so that probably helped to ease some of his concern.

"Levi? You want me to explain?" Aiden's deep velvet voice filled the tense silence.

The other man nodded. "*Ja.* You can do it better than I."

What would he be able to tell the man that may convince him to help them? If he harbored any doubt about their sincerity, she had no doubt he'd be on the phone to the cops ASAP. He looked like the kind of man who took his civic duty seriously. And if he thought Levi was in trouble, or if he thought Celine was in danger, he'd act on it, no matter who Aiden said they were.

Sophie had stepped closer to Aiden again. He couldn't see her, but the scent of her strawberry shampoo grew stronger. Not that he minded, but she was a definite distraction. He pushed his awareness of her to the corner of his mind and stared squarely at Brad. The man meant business, which he respected. Plus, he knew that someone who had spent hours working to fight a fire the night before was someone with integrity, someone who liked to give back to his community.

Aiden could work with that.

He started to reach for his badge and hesitated. Then he scoffed at himself. His cover was blown. Obviously, someone knew who he was, and it was reasonable to assume the secrecy factor was null and void.

He flashed his badge. Brad's eyes narrowed as he scoured the badge like he planned to memorize it. When he appeared satisfied, Aiden returned it to his pocket.

"So, you're a cop."

It was hard to read the inflection in his voice. Was that a statement or a question?

"Yeah, I'm a cop. I'm trying to get these two—" he indicated Sophie and Celine "—to a safe place."

Brad's entire posture stiffened as he pointed to Celine. "Someone's trying to hurt that sweet little girl?"

Celine frowned. She didn't like being called a "sweet little girl" apparently. He held in a smile as Sophie flashed her a warning glance. Sulking, the girl looked away and resumed petting the ecstatic dog.

How much should he tell the guy? Too much information could get him in trouble, too. However, if he didn't give him enough, then the already wary man might call the local cops on them. He needed to find a middle ground between too much and not enough and hope the guy was satisfied with it.

"Okay, Brad, I can tell you this much. Sophie and Celine are in danger. Serious danger. And I am—or I was—working an undercover operation. Levi here, well, he's just a buddy who got caught in the middle when he agreed to help me out. He can vouch for me.

We've known each other for years and even served to-gether."

"True." Levi nodded emphatically. "I would trust Aiden with my life. He's a *gut* man, Brad. *Gut* and hon-est. If he says he's in danger, I believe him."

After a few tense moments, the man shrugged. "If Levi says I can trust you, that's good enough for me. I don't have much room, but I'm okay if you need to bunk down for the night. My wife and my son are both away, so it's good timing."

Aiden glanced at Sophie. She was blinking rapidly. He ran a hand up her arm, intending to comfort her. At his touch, her cheeks flared red. He removed his hand like he'd been shocked.

What was he doing, touching her like that? She was almost a stranger to him. Except she didn't feel like a stranger.

All the adults grinned when Celine let out a huge yawn.

Brad laughed. "I have two spare bedrooms upstairs. My daughter's in college and my son's staying at a friend's house, so they won't be needing them. The la-dies can take the one that belongs to my daughter, and you men can make yourselves comfortable in my son's."

As they headed upstairs, Aiden cast a quick look over his shoulder and saw Brad ambling back to the couch. He cleaned up in the bathroom as best he could. It wasn't dark yet, but he knew that they were all ex-hausted. He wouldn't mind getting to bed early and then heading out again right after breakfast. He still had no clear idea of where they could possibly go.

By the time he reached the bedroom, Levi had already taken up residence on the futon and fallen asleep. Of course, that meant that Aiden had the bed. He sank down on the edge of the mattress. He should pray, he knew that. It was something he did every night without fail before he went to bed. Tonight, however, his mind was a tangled mass of disjointed thoughts. He couldn't seem to focus on a single coherent thought.

He settled for a heartfelt *Stay with us*.

Exhaustion pulled at him. Without a conscious decision, he found himself stretching out the length of the twin bed.

His eyelids were weighted down.

Still, he couldn't drift off without making sure all was well. With a soft groan, he pushed himself off the bed and walked out of the room.

Brad was in the kitchen making himself some macaroni and cheese.

"Hey. I thought you were all out for the night." He nodded toward the elbow macaroni box. "If you're hungry, I can put some more in the pot. It won't be any trouble."

Aiden smiled and shook his head. "No, thanks. Just going to take a quick check around to make sure everything's as it should be."

Skirting the edges of the house, he kept his hand on his service weapon. He wouldn't pull it out unless he needed to, but he was ready. He paused, listening intently to the cacophony of country noises surrounding him. Crickets, the deep-throated croak of bullfrogs echoing from the pond, a dog barking in the distance.

All normal sounds. Nothing suggesting that trouble was coming.

Still, he knew that sometimes trouble came without warning.

Finally satisfied that they were not being watched, Aiden returned to the front of the house and entered. Brad had apparently finished cooking and eating his snack and was back in the living room. The TV was again turned to a news channel. From where he stood, he could see their host flipping through a hunting magazine.

"Night," he called out. "Thanks for letting us trespass."

Brad waved him away. "It's all good. I'll see you in the morning. I don't cook."

Aiden swallowed a chuckle. "We don't expect you to wait on us."

What had awakened him?

Aiden slipped his legs over the edge of the bed and stood slowly, doing his best to be quiet. No sense in Levi waking up if he didn't have to.

Levi shifted, snorting loudly in his sleep.

Aiden grinned. What was he worried about? His buddy could sleep through an explosion.

He slid over to the window and peered out. Not quite dawn yet, but he could see the edge of the horizon beginning to grow lighter.

The desire to see the sunrise moved him to grab his boots and let himself out of the room. In his socks, he stepped silently down the stairs and let himself out the back door onto the patio. He swallowed past the lump in his throat. He had been stuck in the darkness of his false identity for so long, sunrises were no longer part of his day. He had missed that.

"From the rising of the sun unto the going down of the same the Lord's name is to be praised."

The familiar Psalm washed over him. It was a verse in Psalm 113, although the exact number escaped him. It didn't matter, though. What mattered was that the truth that settled in his heart brought him peace. God was with him, through all that had happened and all that was coming.

While he stood in the dew-dampened air, he bent and put his boots on, keeping his face turned toward the horizon. The early morning was hazy, a sheer misty curtain between the horizon and him, but he didn't mind. He wasn't going to miss a second of the glory he'd remembered from the past.

The door creaked open behind him. The scent of strawberries drifted past his nose. He inhaled deeply before he could stop himself. Sophie.

"Couldn't sleep?" He kept his voice at a low murmur, reluctant to intrude on the peace of the moment.

"Nope." Her voice was hushed, too. She moved to his side, her arm brushing his. A tingle shot up his arm. He should move a step or two away from her.

He stayed right where he was.

"My mind is going in a million different directions. Got tired of fighting it." She reached up and pulled the ponytail holder out of her hair, letting it fall around her face. The fragrance of strawberries overwhelmed him.

"Yeah. I get that."

"I should have made coffee."

He smiled. "That would have been nice."

Her gaze focused on the vision blooming before them. The space where the sky and the land touched glowed with pinks and purples. His own gaze was arrested by the awe and wonder reflected in her hazel eyes.

He was in so much trouble.

In the silence, he could hear her breathing as they watched the colors change and the light spill over the land. His fingers twitched, longing searing through him to take her hand in the intimate moment. He shoved both fists into his pockets.

Their peace, and the tension between them, was shattered by loud, clomping footsteps inside the kitchen. Aiden put some distance between himself and Sophie before turning to gauge the situation.

Brad was standing in his robe and sweatpants, making coffee. He nodded at Aiden but didn't speak.

Clearly not a morning person.

The man left the room, and seconds later the sound of the morning news drifted through the screen door.

Sophie sighed.

"What's the plan for today?"

"I'm not completely sure." He sniffed the air. That coffee sure smelled good. "I think if the others don't come down soon on their own, we'll have to wake them."

"Then what?"

He wished he had all the answers she was searching

for. He turned their options over in his mind. "Well, I think it's clear we can't stay here. Nor do I believe it's safe to contact my chief. Not yet. I need to get a burner phone, something that won't be traced to us. Right now, we're too close to where your uncle is. It's only a matter of time before they come looking. That 911 call might have put them off for the time being, because of possible police activity in the area, but it won't keep them away for long."

"So," she began, the studied casualness putting him on alert. "Who is Janet?"

The question knocked the wind out of him for a moment. The temptation to tell her to mind her own business reared up, but he reconsidered. Due to the nature of their partnership, he knew things about her and her family he shouldn't. Telling her about Janet, although distasteful, might be a way to equal things out.

"I don't like to talk about her."

She flushed. "I shouldn't have—"

He held up a hand. "Its fine. She was my fiancée, two years ago. It was a very short-lived engagement. I spent a lot of time on duty. I was still on the evening shift. Cut into my time with her a lot. She didn't like that it hindered our social life." He smiled when she scoffed. "It was also hard because she didn't understand that after something bad or hard happened on duty, I needed time to decompress. I couldn't be happy and funny after someone died. Or after I'd arrested a serial rapist. I just couldn't. So she decided neither could she. She mailed her ring back with a note."

"Mailed it back? Aiden, I think it was a good thing that relationship didn't work out."

He grinned. "Yeah. There's some truth to that."

She nodded and leaned against the railing of the patio. Her hair swished forward to block her face from him as she stared at the ground below. He didn't even think about it, just reached out and brushed the tresses back over her shoulder.

Startled, her gaze shot up to meet his. And stayed there, caught. The electricity they'd both been ignoring hummed.

The door slammed behind them. Aiden jumped back. Sophie's skin flushed to the shade of a ripe strawberry, matching the scent of her hair.

"Sophie!" Celine shouted, eyes terrified. "You guys gotta see what's on TV!"

SEVEN

Sophie charged back into the house, aware of Aiden close on her heels. Her heart thundered as she followed Celine to the living room. Brad was standing in front of the television, pale and wide-awake. He gave her a look of sheer horror when she halted beside him.

And stared.

"What?" Aiden practically shouted at the screen.

The morning news was on, and behind the calm, professional smile of the attractive anchorwoman, were pictures of him and Sophie. The caption read, Drug Dealer and Female Accomplice.

Accomplice for what?

"The police are searching for these two people in connection with the suspicious death of a young man who has been missing since yesterday morning."

Their pictures disappeared and were replaced by a familiar face.

"Cash!" Sophie gasped. Her uncle's employee, the one who had disappointed him.

Aiden's hand landed on her shoulder. She quieted.

"Cash Wellman was reported missing yesterday by his employer, Phillip Larson, a respected businessman in the local area. Mr. Larson stated that the young man failed to report for work," the woman continued.

Sophie's stomach churned. She knew very well that Cash had reported for his job and Phillip had not been happy with him.

The screen shifted to video. A dive team was pulling a body from the river. The camera angle hid the body and the face, but she knew what they had found.

"Two hours ago, his body was pulled from the river. While the coroner hasn't given the cause of death yet, the police appear to be treating this as a homicide."

The camera shifted to the local police representative. "We are taking the death of Cash Wellman very seriously. His employer has informed us that he was last seen in the presence of Adam Steele, a known drug runner, and Larson's own niece, Sophie Larson. Also in their custody is Celine Larson, Sophie Larson's twelve-year-old sister. It is unknown at this time if Sophie is an accomplice or a victim of Adam Steele."

Phillip's handsome face, somber and sincere, replaced the officer's. "I am truly concerned about my nieces. I have heard some terrible things about this Steele fellow. He's very dangerous. My dear nieces are vulnerable, especially Celine, who is deaf. All I want is their safe return."

The television went blank with a click. Brad was standing in front of them, the remote control in one hand and a rifle in the other. It was obvious he knew how to handle the rifle.

Instinctively, Sophie raised her hands and backed away.

"Is it true?" Brad demanded of Aiden. "Did you kill the kid?"

She could barely hear him over the blood pumping in her ears. What if he shot Aiden? Or what if he called the cops, thinking he was helping?

Aiden snorted. His shoulders were relaxed, but his hands were still jammed into his pockets. It looked like they were fisted. For all his casual appearance, he was feeling the tension just as much as the rest of them. He was just more skilled at hiding it. "No, it's not true."

Her gaze bounced to where Brad stood, still not convinced. Of course he wasn't. Why would Aiden admit to killing Cash?

"He didn't kill him. He saved us," Celine blurted out. "That man, our uncle, wants us dead. I don't know why."

Brad's gaze shifted back and forth between them all. If only he would lower the gun.

Levi stepped in the room. "What's going on?"

"We just saw a story on the news," Aiden said, lifting his chin to indicate the television. The sarcasm ringing in his voice was impossible to miss. "It appears that Larson killed an employee and is blaming me. Oh, and I also kidnapped the ladies. So I'm a wanted man."

Brad lowered the gun slightly but didn't set it all the way down. "Well, the little girl doesn't appear to be 'fraid of you."

"I'm not scared of Aiden," Celine declared, arms crossed, eyes zeroed in on Brad's face. She scowled. "I'm not a little girl, either."

"Neither of us fear him," Sophie assured their host. "He's an undercover cop who broke his cover to protect us when I walked in on my uncle in the middle of an illegal meeting."

"Sophie—"

She shot a glare at Aiden. "What could he possibly learn now? Your face is all over the news. We are fugitives and he is holding us at gunpoint."

At that statement, Brad flushed and finally lowered the weapon. "Sorry. I know you guys are in trouble. But this scared me, knowing that someone accused of murder had slept in my house."

Sophie turned to Aiden. "What do we do, Aiden? We can't stay here. It's too close to town and too close to where we were before, when Phillip's men caught up with us. And people in the area will recognize us if we stay too long."

Aiden paced the room, his long strides eating up the room.

"We have to stay underground long enough for my chief to locate the mole in the department. That might be a few days—"

"Or it could be a month!"

He nodded, grimacing. "True. No telling how long these things will take to resolve."

A thick silence descended.

"I know where you can go," Levi announced softly.

"Where?" Sophie and Aiden both demanded, their combined voices loud in the small room.

Levi startled, rocking on his heels a bit.

"Sorry, buddy. Didn't mean to yell," Aiden apologized. A slow tide of color rippled up his neck. Sophie blinked. It was hard to imagine a man as collected as Aiden allowing his control to slip. Or being embarrassed. Yet, clearly, it was happening. This situation was getting to them all.

"Don't worry about it. Look, you need a place where you can go, a place where you can hide and regroup, right?" Levi waited for Aiden's nod. "I have family in Berlin, Ohio. It's a couple of hours from here, but once you get there, who'd think to search for you there?"

Who, indeed? Berlin, Ohio, was known for a booming Amish population. One of the largest in this part of the country.

"That's an Amish area, isn't it?" she asked, just for clarity.

"*Ja.* I'm not Amish anymore, but most of my family is." The pain that blurred his eyes for a moment vanished. She might have been mistaken.

"Levi, we'd stick out in an Amish community," Aiden pointed out.

"You wouldn't if you dressed Plain."

Plain. Amish, no makeup, no jewelry.

No technology.

She looked at Celine. And bit her lip.

"Celine would have to remove her processors." She signed as she spoke so that her sister would be sure to understand completely what was happening.

"What?" Celine's hands flew to the sides of her head, touching the processors. "Why would I have to remove them? Sophie, you know I can't hear anything without them. My ears are dead."

It was true. The surgeries had tunneled through the mastoid bones directly behind her ears so that a thin wire could be inserted into her cochleas, or her inner ears. The receiver was then implanted in the bone itself. The effect was that Celine now had access to enough speech sounds that she was able to understand and participate in most conversations around her. Unfortunately, the surgeries that allowed her to hear with her processors also destroyed all residual hearing, which meant without the technology, she had two completely dead ears.

Sophie couldn't even comprehend how terrified her sister must feel at the thought of having all hearing stripped from her while someone was trying to kill them.

She moved toward Celine. Aiden was faster. He placed his hands on her shoulders and looked down into her pale face.

"Celine, your sister and I will be with you the whole time. I know you're scared. But I promise you, I won't let anyone hurt you. Your safety is the most important thing to me."

"Are you scared?" she asked Aiden.

Sophie's heart beat against her ribs. The backs of her eyes stung. She hated to see her sister so tortured.

She was also shocked to see Aiden nod in response. The men she had known in her life would never have shown vulnerability by admitting fear.

"I am scared, Celine. I think we'd be foolish not to be. But fear can keep you alert."

"How do you... I mean—" She looked at Sophie.

"I think Celine is trying to understand how you cope with your fear." She raised her eyebrow at her sister to ask if she was correctly interpreting the half-asked question.

"Exactly."

The sudden bright smile transformed Aiden's face. He was a nice-looking man. Her breath stalled, and his smile seemed to grab hold of her very heart.

"I'm never alone. Even when everything seems dark and scary, I know that God is near. That's how I survive."

God. Of course. She'd let her relationship with Him take a back seat for so long. Yet, here was a man who lived by his wits daily, boldly proclaiming faith in a way that made shame sink into her skin. When had she grown so lax?

First she let her family down, then God.

No wonder Celine was scared. She didn't understand that her sister was in this for the long haul. Or that she would put her first.

"Celine, Aiden's right." She stepped up beside him. "We will keep you safe. You are our priority."

A sarcastic sneer shadowed her sister's face. "You say that now, but you practically abandoned us when you graduated."

Okay. She deserved that. "I know."

She could see she'd shocked her sister.

"Really?"

"Yeah. I did get too caught up in my career. I should have made more of an effort." The tears that had been threatening overwhelmed her and leaked out. She knuckled them away from her eyes. "I lost so much time with Mom and Dad. Brian was the only one I really kept consistent contact with, and now he's gone. I didn't make time for you, but that's done. From now on, you will always be more important than my career."

Aiden's warm arm, which was looped around her shoulder, was a blanket of peace and comfort. For a moment, she basked in that peace. Then she stepped forward to give her sister a quick hug, dislodging the arm. She missed it immediately but knew that it was better not to rely on Aiden too much.

She had promised her sister to put her first.

It was a plan she intended to keep. But in order to do that, she needed to get her out of this mess alive.

She had no idea how to do that with their uncle still free.

Aiden let his arm fall to his side and watched Sophie embrace her sister. It felt empty now that it wasn't wrapped around her.

Ridiculous. He scowled. There was no way he was letting this craziness continue. He'd get the sisters to safety, put their uncle behind bars, then he was out of their lives.

To distract himself from the hollow ache the plan left inside his heart, he turned back to Levi.

"You okay?" Levi asked.

His friend was much too observant.

"I will be. I need to finish this."

Fortunately, Levi didn't ask what he was referring to.

He wasn't sure if he could have completely answered that question.

"Why don't we pack up and I'll lead you—"

At this point, Aiden held up a hand. Levi faltered and fell silent.

"What?"

"Levi, I don't think you should come with us. Actually, I know you shouldn't." He was aware of Sophie's presence.

What would he do if he led his friend into danger, too?

"Is it safe for him to stay?" Suddenly Sophie was back at his side. "If they know we were at his house, wouldn't he still be at risk?"

How had he not considered that? The magnitude of his failure stunned him. "You're right. Not only that, but our phones were left in his grass out in the field. Levi, man, I—"

The other man waved his words away. "It doesn't matter. We have always helped each other—it didn't matter if it was dangerous. It's not like I've never faced trouble before."

The reference to their joint military experiences washed over him. He pushed away the encroaching darkness that threatened to swallow him, dragging in a deep breath and thrusting his unsteady hands deep into his pockets. With a silent prayer for help, he forced his attention to remain focused on the present. Levi was a bit pale, as well. He rarely let down his guard enough for those memories to surface.

His glance shifted over to focus on Brad. The owner of the house seemed troubled.

"Brad?"

Brad shrugged. "I feel like I should apologize. I trust Levi and I trust his judgment."

Aiden nodded. He knew there was more on the man's mind.

Brad sighed. "I let you folks stay for the night. It was the right thing to do. I feel bad that I'm relieved you're going. You're in trouble. I want to help. I do. But you need to leave. My wife will be coming home in a few days. And my son will be home today. If it was just me here, I'd let you stay. But I will not put my family in jeopardy."

Sophie moved closer, her scent tickling his nose, distracting him. "We do appreciate your kindness. I hope your wife won't mind that we were here."

His face softened as he looked at the pretty woman standing so close to Aiden. "She won't mind, ma'am. But that's how she is. I won't have her in danger."

There was nothing he could say to that. A man had a right to protect his family. He would have thought less of the man if he didn't take his responsibilities seriously.

"I understand. We'll be out of your hair as soon as we can." They'd have to plan on the road. "I need everyone to get all their gear together, what there is of it. Wash up, brush your teeth if you can. Who knows how long it will be before you can brush them again."

At least they'd all had showers. That was one thing in their favor.

It took them another half hour to gather up what they

needed. Brad met them at the door with a small back-pack. If he were to guess, he'd say the man was feeling guilty about kicking them out.

"It's not much." Brad handed the backpack to Aiden. "I made some peanut butter and jelly sandwiches, put in some granola bars and mixed nuts and four bottled waters."

Aiden shrugged into the shoulder straps. "It's more than we had. Appreciate your kindness."

Nodding, Brad turned to Levi. "Stop in when you are back home. In the meantime, I'll drive by your place once a day. Check on things. Get the mail."

"*Gut*. I'll see you soon."

By now, all Aiden wanted was to be on the way. The spot between his shoulders tingled as if he had a target on his back. In a way he did. They all did. The farther away they traveled the safer he'd feel.

And maybe he'd be able to get a phone to contact the chief. Get an update on the situation. Until then, he had to keep going.

"Should we take my truck?" Levi asked as they began to walk out the door. "It's just a short walk to the field where we left it."

Aiden thought for a moment. It was tempting, but he rejected the idea. "No. I think it would draw too much attention. It's our last known vehicle. I don't think we can risk it."

"Wait!" Brad shouted. "I have an old vehicle that we were saving for the crash-up derby in August. It's still registered, and my son isn't using it at the moment. It's not perfect, but it will get you where you need to go."

Aiden spun around. "Does it still drive safely?"

He wouldn't get his hopes up, though a car would certainly help.

"Yes, sir." Brad pulled a key off the key rack hanging on the wall. Aiden had never seen so many key rings. How many vehicles did the man own?

Five, it turned out.

And one of them was a 2001 Jeep Cherokee. It might have been dark blue, but it was so dirty the color was hard to tell for sure. There were several dents and dings in it, but it looked decent enough for their purposes.

"This just might do the trick. I can't pay you for it now, but—"

Brad waved that away. "Don't worry about it. My kid got a new truck recently, and this was literally just taking up space."

Wordlessly, Aiden reached out and shook Brad's hand. He wasn't sure he was capable of speech at the moment. The man's generosity overwhelmed him. Brad tossed him the key with a wink.

Aiden held the back passenger door open. Levi stopped him.

"I'll drive."

"Huh?"

"It wasn't my face on the television screen."

Oh.

"Aiden, do you think you and I should ride in the back?" Sophie asked.

Shrugging, Aiden gestured for her to get in the back seat. "It makes sense. He and Celine will be less noticeable."

She didn't look happy, even though it had been her idea. She probably didn't like the thought of her sister being so visible. Her pretty mouth was pulled down in a frown. He admired how protective she was of Celine.

Good grief. He needed to stop thinking about her before he got into more trouble than he was already in.

Sophie slid in and he followed suit. Levi and Celine strapped themselves into the front seat. When Levi turned the key, the shriek that issued from engine was anything but comforting. Levi let the motor die.

Brad scratched his head. "Yeah, there's a trick to it. Hold down the brake and the gas at the same time."

Levi did. Sophie latched on to Aiden's hand as the Jeep coughed and choked before catching. The engine roared to life. This car was inconspicuous? Maybe if they could avoid shutting off the engine.

Brad knocked on the hood. "You're all set." He waved and sauntered back to the house.

Levi turned in his seat. "Aiden?"

"It's fine. We have no other option." His jaw hurt. He hadn't realized he was clenching his teeth. It might have been humorous if they weren't running for their lives.

But they were. And every minute idle was one that they'd never get back.

"We gotta go."

Levi nodded. Facing the front, he jerked the car into Reverse. Aiden's head whipped forward. When the car was in Drive, he turned to look at Sophie. She was laughing and shaking her head.

"What?" he whispered.

She nodded her head at Levi, still chuckling.

"Yeah, he learned to drive at a late age. Still learning, in fact."

"Funny, I heard that," Levi called back.

His hand was still joined with Sophie's. He should pull away. But he didn't.

Instead, he held tighter. Her face was turned toward the window. What was she thinking? Her shoulders were tight, hunched. That wasn't good. She was either furious, scared or both.

He didn't know what else he could have done to get them to safety quicker. He shifted in his seat. Was she blaming him for their current situation? A joking comment rose to his lips, his normal reaction when he felt uncomfortable. He swallowed it. Now was not the time for humor.

In the front seat, Levi turned on the radio. A country music song burst through the speakers. Figured. Not a fan of that particular genre, Aiden rolled his eyes. When Levi began to sing along enthusiastically, Aiden squeezed his face into a grimace.

Sophie smiled when Celine giggled.

Aiden took advantage of the music and asked, "Sophie, how are you holding up?"

She shrugged. "As good as you'd expect."

That wasn't much of an answer, although he understood it.

"I'm sorry we're in this mess."

Her eyes widened. She glanced quickly to the two in the front. When she spoke again, it was in a low voice. He leaned closer to hear her. "You can't be thinking any of this is your fault."

"Isn't it? I led you and Levi right into a trap."

She snorted. "Because you're to blame for my uncle being cruel and greedy? No." She bit her lip. "I think if either of us is to blame, it's me."

"How do you figure?"

Her cheeks flushed. When she lowered her eyes, she appeared to notice that their hands were still joined. Turning the shade of a ripe tomato, she jerked her hand away from his.

"It's my fault because I let my career get in the way of my family. Maybe if I had been closer, maybe I would have been home and been able to help."

"If you had been home, you'd be dead. And Celine would be in foster care. Or in Phillip's custody."

The idea of that vulgar monster having control of sweet little Celine churned his stomach. If he failed, the woman beside him and the giggling girl up front would pay for it.

Not on his watch.

He'd been focused on nailing Phillip Larson to avenge his partner. That remained important to him. But now he had another reason to see the man locked up.

Make that two reasons.

And they were both sitting here in the car with him.

EIGHT

"Aiden? Are you all right?" Sophie's voice tugged him out of the darkness filling his heart. He shot her a grin he was far from feeling.

She responded with a fierce frown. Apparently, it wasn't a convincing grin.

"I'm fine, Soph. Don't worry about me."

She huffed out an exasperated breath. "Don't worry about you? You lost all color. What is it with men? You know, there's nothing wrong with acknowledging something's wrong."

Being lumped into the category of all men didn't sit well with him.

But he wasn't ready to talk about his feelings. He nearly snickered as he thought of how the guys back at the police department would razz him about getting sentimental. Not happening.

"Seriously. I'm good."

She shook her head and faced the window again. He could tell he'd offended her by his answer, but what did she expect? They barely knew each other.

He glanced out his window.

"Levi! Pull into this mall!"

Without hesitation, Levi obeyed, spinning the wheel so fast that Sophie slid into Aiden's side.

"Oomph!" She knocked the breath out of him. He couldn't tell if it was the collision or her sudden closeness. He was probably better off not exploring that line of thinking. She shifted back to her side before he could finish his thought.

Levi had neglected to flip on his blinker. The car behind them leaned on the horn. Aiden couldn't blame him. Levi stopped the car in a parking space and switched off the radio.

"Okay. Why are we here?" Sophie asked.

Aiden pointed at the Super Center ahead of them. "Perfect place to pick up a couple of pay-as-you-go phones. We can contact my chief. And we can also contact Brad, see if he noticed anything on the radio or television."

"But what if Phillip's men are listening in to their phones?"

He reached out and squeezed her hand, releasing it before she could pull away.

"These phones are really hard to track. We'll buy an extra one, just in case, but I think we should be safe."

"That's an awful lot of money to waste."

He nodded. "It is. But I'm sure when this is over, the department will reimburse the expenses. We'll have to use cash. We don't want a trace on credit cards."

"How will we buy them?" She pulled the band out of her hair, fluffed it and then smoothed her hair back into a ponytail, quickly securing it with the band. The sight of her hair spilling around her face momentarily distracted him from the conversation. "Our pictures have been all over the news."

"Huh? Oh, yeah. Well," he said, meeting his buddy's eyes in the mirror. "Wanna go shopping, Levi?"

"No, but I will."

Honest to a fault.

"Let's see how much cash we have."

Sophie pulled out a rectangular object from her pocket. Looking closer, he chuckled. Instead of a wallet, she had dollar bills wrapped around her driver's license and several other cards, which were secured with a rubber band.

"I have forty-eight dollars," Levi called back from his seat.

Sophie unraveled her bills, counted them and handed them over. There was no hesitation on her part. The trust she showed left him humbled and awed. "I have almost two hundred."

"You normally carry around that much?"

"Nope." She flicked her gaze toward Celine. "I was traveling."

"Ah. Got it." He counted his own cash. "I have another hundred and sixty."

He handed the money to Levi. "Get the three cheapest phones and plans—"

"Wait!" Celine shouted. "I have some money."

The girl pulled out a wad of bills and shoved them at Levi without counting them. "I was saving for some new jeans, but you can have it."

His vision blurred. Clearing the sudden obstruction from his throat, he tapped her shoulder. She glanced his way. "Thanks, kid. It will really help out."

No one commented on how rough his voice was.

Sophie was fighting her own battle with tears. He pretended to be really focused on putting his wallet away to give her time to recover her composure.

"Right. I'll be back," Levi said, pocketing the money and then heading for the store, whistling as he went.

"You know," Sophie commented, "that man is completely off-key."

"He knows." Aiden leaned back against the seat, keeping low. "I sometimes think he does it on purpose."

She snickered, and the soft sound made him smile.

"I'm hungry," Celine announced.

"We have those granola bars. Or do you want a sandwich?" Sophie rooted around inside the backpack, then held out her hands for Celine to choose.

"A sandwich. Of course."

"You want one?" Sophie held one out to Aiden.

"Sure." As he took the baggie with the sandwich inside, their fingers touched. This time, he expected the jolt of electricity that sparked between them. Was it his imagination, or did her fingers linger against his?

He pulled back, dropping his eyes to his food as if he was starving. For a few minutes, chewing was the only sound in the car.

When they were finished eating, they sat in silence waiting for Levi.

Ten minutes later, the front driver's-side door opened

and Levi joined them. He pointed at the empty sandwich bags. "Save one for me?"

"Nah. We ate them all. Of course, we saved you one." He tossed a sandwich to his friend. Levi handed him the bag with the phones in exchange. He wasted no time in dumping them out of the bag and using his pocketknife to tear open the packages.

"Need any help?"

He handed the phone he'd freed to Sophie. "If you can start setting that one up, it would help a lot."

"No problem."

It took them almost twenty minutes, but they were able to get all the phones programmed. Aiden sighed. Now they were in business.

"What's in the other bag?" Celine asked.

"Other bag?" Aiden looked up at Levi. He'd been so focused on Sophie he hadn't noticed that Levi was carrying more than one bag.

Levi hefted the plastic bag up so they could see it. "I thought it might be a good idea to buy a few more snacks. It was a *gut* idea, right?"

"A very good idea. Most of the food we have is already gone." Sophie reached for the bag and put the contents into the backpack she was holding. "We have no idea when we'll be able to buy more food."

"True." Aiden handed one of the phones back up to the front seat. "Why don't you call Brad and see if anything is happening?"

Levi took the phone and punched in a phone number. "Speaker?"

"Yeah, you better. It would save time."

Hopefully, Brad wouldn't say anything that would scare Celine.

The phone rang. "He might not pick up if he doesn't know the number. I wouldn't," Sophie mused.

She was right. It went to voice mail.

"Leave a message," Aiden told him reluctantly. As much as he didn't want to, if Brad wouldn't answer, there wasn't really a choice.

Doubt flickered over Levi's face before his expression smoothed out. "Hello, Brad. It's me—"

The phone was abruptly answered. "Don't say your name!" Brad yelled into the receiver.

Aiden shot up in his seat and grabbed the phone from Levi. "What's happened?"

The command in his voice seemed to have a calming influence on Brad.

"My son came home early. I was in the shower and didn't hear him come in until it was too late."

"Too late? Too late for what?" Impatience bit at him. He ground his teeth to keep from barking at the man.

"He went out to the garage and saw that his car was gone. No one drives that thing. Not since he bought his truck. I didn't think he'd pay any attention to it. I came downstairs to hear him on the phone. He had called the cops to report it had been stolen."

Sophie's jaw dropped. Levi lowered his head into his hands. Aiden stared at the phone in horror. The urge to bang his head against the top of the seat came and went. It would serve no purpose.

"Have the police connected the missing car to us?" he grated out.

"Man, I have no clue. I made myself scarce when they came. Made up some kind of errand. I couldn't lie to them, and I was afraid if I said that Levi had the car, they'd have his picture up on news, too."

A few seconds later, he disconnected the call.

"Now what?"

Aiden cast his gaze at Sophie. She was so calm, so trusting. A man could live for a week off the look she gave him.

He shook his head, trying to shake the attraction that continued to dog him despite the horrific circumstances. Then he took a moment to consider their next move. He sighed. No one was going to like what he had to say.

"Ditch the vehicle. We go on foot from here."

On foot? Sophie blinked, hoping that he wasn't serious.

"Do we just leave the car here?" she asked cautiously.

"No. It's too obvious here. Besides, we'd be vulnerable if we started walking around here. Let's drive and find a more secluded spot to leave it."

Any hopes that he was kidding died right there. Still, she didn't protest. He was doing what he could to keep them safe and alive. She wasn't sure why it had happened so fast, but her trust in him was absolute.

Lord, thank You for providing a protector like Aiden. Please keep us safe and help him to heal from whatever wounds he's suffering from.

It was so clear to her that he was suffering.

If they had time, she'd try to talk with him about it. As it was, they barely had time to breathe. They drove to a park and ride near the edge of town, one that had not been taken care of very well. There were only two other vehicles parked in it, their drivers nowhere in sight.

"We'll leave the car here. Let's not dawdle, folks." Aiden took the backpack and slung it over one shoulder. He pulled out a map that was stuck in the driver's door pocket. "Which way to your relatives' house, Levi?"

Celine snuggled up to Sophie's side while the men held a brief discussion about the route they should take. She pulled her sister close and kissed the top of her head.

"Will we be okay?" Celine signed to her.

Biting her lip, Sophie considered her answer. As much as she wanted to comfort her sibling, she didn't think lying to her was the way to deal with her fears. Her eyes slid to Aiden. Warmth drizzled down her spine and filled her with a sense of peace.

She knew how to answer.

"I don't know what will happen," she signed to her sister. "What I do know is that God is on our side. He sent us Aiden to get us safely away before Phillip could hurt us." She deliberately skipped calling him uncle. The less they dwelt on their relationship with that monster, the happier they would both be.

"Do you believe He hears us?"

"Absolutely." She'd ignored Him in her pursuit of her career. That was the wrong thing to do, but her faith was reawakening, burning quietly inside. She might have left Him behind when she went in search of success and independence, but God had been faithful and hadn't abandoned her. He wouldn't do so now, either.

"Sophie, Celine, are you ladies ready?" Aiden asked. She nudged her sister forward.

The small group moved out at a brisk pace. Without any conscious planning, they realigned themselves until Celine was walking up near Levi and Sophie was striding beside Aiden. For a while, no one spoke. Partly, she mused, because they were vulnerable and didn't want to draw attention to themselves.

She tripped on a root and would have gone flying were it not for the strong hand that snatched her back to an upright position.

"Thanks," she murmured to her silent companion.

He nodded once, a small crooked smile playing about his mouth.

That was another reason not to talk. The terrain was anything but smooth. They needed to pay attention to where they were setting their feet down. After half an hour of walking, however, she was willing to risk a few bruises. The fear screaming inside her made the silence almost unbearable.

"How long will this journey take?" Levi was probably the one to ask, but she didn't want to talk any louder than necessary. She kept her eyes on the ground and sensed his shrug.

"Not sure. Traveling on foot is not the best or quickest way to do it."

"You haven't called your chief yet." They'd been so keen on escaping she'd forgotten the reason he'd wanted the phones in the first place.

"Not had the time. And I really want to put some distance between us and your uncle before I call."

She thought for a moment.

"You're procrastinating," she realized.

"Procrastinating? Why would I do that?"

His defensive tone told her she was right.

"You don't know if you really want to know who the mole is."

He didn't deny it. Nor did he admit it.

"Aiden?"

He sighed. "Do we have to do this? Right now?" he practically growled at her.

She widened the distance between them. Honestly, she wasn't trying to offend him. All she wanted was some basic conversation to keep her mind occupied so that it would stop chasing after worst-case scenarios. Her anxiety levels were climbing by the minute. The muscles in her neck were so tight it felt like turning her head would be disastrous.

"Sophie, I didn't mean to snarl."

She sniffed.

"Oh, come on. We've been through a rough couple of days. Cut me some slack here."

It was true. They had come through a harrowing time, were still going through it. And it was largely due to Aiden that they had survived it.

She slowed, feeling petty.

"You're right. I'm overreacting."

His hand brushed her shoulder. "I think you've got just cause. You've been so strong. I wish I could tell you we could stop, and that things would go back to normal. But we can't. Not yet. For now, all we can do is keep going."

Afraid her voice would wobble if she spoke, she contented herself with a nod. She wasn't sure she even knew what normal looked like anymore. It had never crossed her mind when she was climbing the career ladder that she would one day soon be without her parents and brother or that she would be a parent to her sassy little sister.

Reality was hard.

The awkward moment was shattered by a phone ringing. Sophie put a hand to her chest, as if that would slow her racing heart. Celine went a few steps before she realized the others had stopped. The ringtone was too high for her to hear.

"Yeah," Aiden answered.

She heard the man on the other end yelling. Aiden paled as he put the call on speaker. "Say that again."

"You've been spotted!" Brad repeated. "The call came in over my pager. Some woman claims she saw you in a store parking lot. There are going to be checkpoints on the main road. It's a manhunt."

Aiden hit a button, disconnecting the call.

Sophie stepped closer and lowered her voice, even though there was no one else around. "What do we do now?"

In response, he pulled out the map. She tapped her foot, waiting for him to finish examining the paper and inform them of the new plan of action.

"There." Aiden jabbed the map with his finger. "We'll head for the river and follow it."

The river.

A swift pulse of sheer terror swept through her. Then

common sense reasserted itself. They were going to walk near the river. Near it. Aiden had said nothing about going in it.

Because even if it was the calmest trickling brook, she didn't know if she could do it.

She pulled in a deep breath, steadying herself.

Aiden's hand found her shoulder again and slid gently until it was cupping the side of her neck.

"Sophie?" His deep voice calmed her frazzled nerves. She risked a glance up into his dark eyes and stayed. The assurance and promise she read in them healed something in her she hadn't even realized was broken.

Aiden would make sure no harm came to her or Celine.

"I'm good, Aiden." When his eyebrow lifted, doubting her, she lifted her chin. She was strong enough to deal with her fears. They weren't going to slow the group down. "I'm fine. I don't like water, but we'll be walking near it, not going for a swim."

He searched her face. When his gaze settled momentarily on her lips before moving back to her eyes, her breath hitched. The moment stretched out, neither of them moving.

"You guys coming, or are you just gonna stand there?" Celine's tone carried a touch of sarcasm.

She grinned. Trust her sister to break up a tense moment.

"We're coming! Hold your horses," she called back.

Aiden's hand dropped from her neck. Disappointment zinged through her.

They resumed walking. Although they were no longer touching, she was aware of the man beside her with every step.

Her sense of peace dissipated two hours later. Levi and Celine were still up ahead of them, but her sister's steps had begun to drag, and Levi was limping slightly. Was it an old injury, or had he injured himself on their trek?

It was Aiden who worried her, though. He had retreated into silence, his expression growing dark and grim. She knew very little about him. What was going on behind the handsome mask?

Sophie was so deep in her musings that the sound didn't penetrate at first.

Slowly she became aware of a muted rushing roar. Her legs stiffened and her hands shook as the reality of what she was hearing sank in.

They were at the river. And the path they were walking was no longer smooth.

It was rocky and twisted.

And narrow.

"We'll have to go single file in places, but we'll be fine," Aiden commented.

She could do this.

Her stomach was twisted into a tight knot.

Years of panic bubbled up inside her. It had been years since she'd nearly drowned as a teenager. The nightmares had stopped long ago, but now, faced with the swift current of the river, all the fear she'd felt that day flooded her mind. She remembered the feeling of being trapped under the water, knowing she was going to die.

How could she walk so close to the water? The path was so narrow, it would be too easy to fall into the churning water. All she wanted to do was run the other direction.

But she couldn't. If she didn't get past her fear, she'd be putting the lives of those she cared about—Celine, Aiden and Levi—at risk.

She had no choice.

Dear Reader,

Your opinions are important to us. So if you'll participate in our fa
and free "One Minute" Survey, **YOU** can pick up to four wonderf\
books that **WE** pay for!

As a leading publisher of women's fiction, we'd love to hear from
you. That's why we promise to reward you for completing our
survey.

IMPORTANT: Please complete the survey and return it. We'll ser
your Free Books and Free Mystery Gifts right away. **And we pay**
for shipping and handling too! *We pay for*
EVERYTHING!

Try **Love Inspired® Romance Larger-Print** books and fall in love
with inspirational romances that take you on an uplifting journey
faith, forgiveness and hope.

Try **Love Inspired® Suspense Larger-Print** books where courage
and optimism unite in stories of faith and love in the face of dang

Or TRY BOTH!

Thank you again for participating in our "One Minute"
Survey. It really takes just a minute (or less) to complete the
survey… and your free books and gifts will be well worth it!

Sincerely,

Pam Powers

Pam Powers
for Reader Service

"One Minute" Survey

GET YOUR FREE BOOKS AND FREE GIFTS!

✓ Complete this Survey   ✓ Return this survey

1 Do you try to find time to read every day?
☐ YES   ☐ NO

2 Do you prefer books which reflect Christian values?
☐ YES   ☐ NO

3 Do you enjoy having books delivered to your home?
☐ YES   ☐ NO

4 Do you find a Larger Print size easier on your eyes?
☐ YES   ☐ NO

YES! I have completed the above "One Minute" Survey. Please send me my Free Books and Free Mystery Gifts (worth over $20 retail). I understand that I am under no obligation to buy anything, as explained on the back of this card.

☐ I prefer Love Inspired® Romance Larger Print 122/322 IDL GNTG

☐ I prefer Love Inspired® Suspense Larger Print 107/307 IDL GNTG

☐ I prefer BOTH 122/322 & 107/307 IDL GNTS

FIRST NAME   LAST NAME

ADDRESS

APT.#   CITY

STATE/PROV.   ZIP/POSTAL CODE

READER SERVICE—Here's how it works:

NINE

Whatever Sophie was thinking about, it couldn't be good.

Her face had grown chalk white. So pale, he thought she was ready to faint. Even the easy lope of her walk had changed. When she halted completely, he was ready for it.

"Sophie."

He had to call her name twice before she answered him. When her eyes lifted to his, it was a punch in the gut. The terror blazing in her hazel glance was no mere fear of water.

"I really don't like water."

Suddenly Celine was there. He'd been so concerned with Sophie he'd forgotten about Celine and Levi. Celine took Sophie's hand in hers.

That jolted Sophie out of her daze. Her gaze became intense as she turned it on her sister and her mouth tightened. He could feel the resolution pouring from her.

"I'm okay."

"We'll find another way—" Aiden said.

She shook her head, stopping his words in their tracks.

"We'll do this. It's the best way. I'm not going to let a fear of the water hold us back."

Celine watched her sister. After a moment, she nodded and turned back to start walking. The kid was seriously impressing him with her gumption.

He wished he could take Sophie's hand to comfort her, but the path was too narrow. He stayed at her shoulder.

"You can't swim?"

She snorted out a short mocking laugh.

"That's the irony. Yes, I can swim." Her shoulders shrugged. "I went canoeing once with a group of friends. I'd never gone before, so I had no clue what to expect. When the canoe tipped over, I wasn't prepared. I was trapped under it and had no air. Breathed in some water before they got me out. I've avoided water since."

Listening to her voice, he could find no trace of panic now.

It hit him hard. She was ignoring her own fear, had deliberately shoved it aside in order to protect them. Admiration for her rose.

The river came into view. It was awesome to see the power of the rapids. He knew this river was famous for its white-water rafting tours. He'd even been on a few. When he was younger, he'd trained as a tour guide and spent a couple of summers working on the Youghiogheny River. It had been a great time, but not something for anyone who had a phobia of water.

A few pebbles came loose under Celine's foot as she stumbled. Sophie lurched forward, but Levi was there to steady the child. Aiden put his hand on the small of Sophie's back. "Levi will protect her."

Just like I will protect you. Lord, protect us, guide us, and please help us to escape those who would harm us.

"I trust you."

Those simple words were a balm to his wounded spirit. And a warning. Trust was one thing, and he prayed he would be deserving of it. The other thing— the attraction that was building between them—was not something he could allow to continue. He'd been trying to ignore it, but he was failing to control it. He'd never talked about his sister to anyone other than Levi. Not even to his partner.

He wanted to talk to Sophie, though. He wanted her to understand him. And he needed her to understand why he could never act on the attraction between them.

Just not now. Right now, he needed to keep them all alive. He said another prayer, asking God for wisdom.

The shrill ring of his phone blasted through the silence. Above him, the leaves rustled as birds were startled out of the trees.

The only person who had this number was Brad. It couldn't be good.

"Another call went out on my pager. They're bringing in dogs."

Dogs. To track their scent.

It didn't matter where they walked. Dogs would be able to trace them. And the dogs were faster than people.

It was only a matter of time.

However, even if dogs were tracking them, they

could travel faster on water. Hopefully, they'd be able to get out of the river at a spot that was hard to get cars to. It was, truly, their only shot at evading capture.

But Sophie had a terror of the water. He couldn't ask her to go in the water. But he didn't have a choice. They were out of options.

"I'm sorry—"

She already knew what he was going to say. He could see it in the stillness of her face as she looked at him.

"We're going in there, aren't we?" She pointed to the river.

"If I can find a way for us to do it. It's not swimmable here."

Her lips tilted upward although the smile didn't touch her eyes. "Is swimmable a real word?"

"It is now. Who decides who's allowed to make up words?"

She chuckled softly. He nodded. Both of them knew the conversation was to take the edge off the anxiety hovering over them.

They walked on for another half hour. Aiden scoured the river and the surrounding area, searching for a way that they could get across the river. If they could just reach the other side, it would break their scents up. There, up ahead. What was that?

Hope sprouted in his soul. This might work.

"Look over there." He pointed to the abandoned raft sitting on the side of the river. She bit her lip but did not reply.

"Levi, Celine." He waited until they turned around. Not caring who saw, he grabbed one of Sophie's hands and held it close. It was trembling and cold, but her eyes were resolute. She would do whatever he asked her to do to protect her sister.

Had to admire that.

"They're bringing dogs. We have to get in the water." His heart ached at the way the kid's face paled. If only there was another way.

There wasn't.

"There's a raft down there."

"Do you know how to work one of those?" Sophie asked. One would never know how terrified she was. He could feel it in her hands, although her face was still.

"I do. I was a white-water rafting guide for two years. I'll get you through this. We don't need to do the whole river. I just want to get us far enough down that when we come out on the other side, the dogs won't be able to find us."

At least, he hoped they wouldn't. Once they were far enough away, he'd take a chance on contacting his chief.

He led them down to the raft. Inspecting it thoroughly, he was relieved to see that whoever had abandoned it had left two oars with it. When he was convinced that the craft was sturdy, he gave them a quick demonstration of how to sit balanced on the edge with a foot wedged under the inflated log-shaped items anchored in the middle. People often thought those were to sit on, but they were really to help the raft keep its shape.

When Celine removed the processors from either side of her head and handed them to her sister to store in the backpack, pity, mingled with an additional dose of dread, surged through him.

His job to protect her would be more complicated if she couldn't hear. He recalled what she'd said. She couldn't hear anything without them.

"Levi."

Levi nodded. "I will not be able to row. Not with this arm."

"Can you handle it?" he whispered to Sophie.

Her chin rose a notch. "I will do whatever you need me to do."

He accepted her answer. "Okay, let me go through the commands."

He showed her how to row, and then what the different calls he'd say would mean. He knew they needed to hurry, but this was too important to skip. Going into the water without basic knowledge could be deadly. It was also important for her to have some feeling of control. Giving her a task and directions could be the difference between success and failure. Which wasn't an option. Failure meant injury or worse.

"Everyone ready?" He shoved off and then climbed into the raft. "Forward!"

Sophie picked up her oar and paddled the way he'd shown her, her strokes strong and sure. Only the tightness in her posture showed how terrified she truly was.

They were approaching another rapid. He needed to gauge it right so they didn't get caught on a rock. "Back!"

She reversed the oar.

"Stop!" He shouted, lifting his voice above the crashing water around them. She lifted the oar out of the water.

The raft lifted, then dropped and bounced as they hit the rapid. Icy water crashed over them. He shook it from his eyes. No one had fallen out, and he would take that as a win. They were far from out of danger, though, so he kept alert.

He paddled quickly, pushing hard to swerve the raft around the rock. It brushed up against the large boulder. Celine bobbed on her seat. Levi caught her.

Aiden grimaced. Then they were past. One down. Unfortunately, there were many more to come. Setting his jaw, he poured all his energy into the task of maneuvering the dangerous waters.

The water beside them exploded with a loud blast. A second later, a bullet bounced off a nearby rock.

He shouted to Levi to get Celine down as he dove for Sophie. Sophie screamed as she lost her balance and began to topple off the edge of the raft.

She was going in! Sucking in a deep breath, she closed her eyes to keep the water out.

Strong hands gripped her upper arms and dragged her back onto the raft. Instead of sitting on the edge, she found herself pushed into the interior, shoved up against the inflated cushion. She craned her head and nearly cried with relief when she saw that Celine was uninjured. Scared, absolutely, but unharmed.

A litany of thanksgiving fell from her lips, praising God for His care.

It was cut off by a shriek as another shot rang out.

"We're being shot at!" she yelled.

"It's not the police," Aiden yelled back.

Which was much worse. Phillip's men had found them. "How did they find us?"

"Probably the same way that Brad knew we were in danger."

The mole. Someone had a pager or access to police channels. They must have alerted Phillip to the search and the location.

Before she could think too deeply about the situation, they hit another rapid. She refused to allow Aiden to do all the work. Pushing herself back up on the edge, she shoved her foot into the crevice on the side to secure herself then grabbed her oar, which had fallen to the floor. Aiden frowned, but didn't protest. How could he? He needed another person to paddle, and she was the best one for the job. The cold water smashing into them and the boulders they had to skirt kept her from getting bogged down in her own panic.

She'd almost fallen in, and he had protected her. Just as he had promised he would.

They came out of the second rapid none the worse.

They could do this.

Another shot rang out and Levi shouted, clutching at his shoulder. Red bloomed out and spread across his shirt. Celine cried out and sobbed.

"Levi!" Aiden bellowed.

"I'm *gut*. Don't worry about me."

Except his pallor belied his words. He was losing blood and would need attention fast.

She glanced back at the shoreline. The two men shooting at them were trying to run along the rocky land beside the river. Not with much success, she was relieved to note. Nor with any sort of speed. The rough terrain prevented that. She risked another glance back to check their progress. The man in the lead tripped and tumbled into the water. He managed to catch himself on a branch before the flowing current carried him more than a few feet. His partner caught up with him and helped him, sputtering and choking, to shore. Their mingled shouts were drowned out by the roar made by the mighty river.

His face a grim mask, Aiden continued to paddle. Sophie followed his lead. Until they were out of the water, there was little they could do to help Levi.

After continuing to fight their way through the rapids one at a time, they lost sight of the men.

Had they passed the police blockade? Or had the dogs followed the scent to the river?

As if reading her thoughts, Aiden called out, "We need to go downstream far enough to get beyond the dogs. I'm hoping it will take them a while to pick up the scent again, especially since they don't know where we'll get off."

Which made sense. Aiden didn't even know where they would exit the water. It needed to be soon. Her eyes rested on Levi.

"I think he's going into shock. We need to get him warm."

Her own teeth were chattering from the freezing water. The bottom of the raft was drenched, as was their clothing. Getting him to a safe, dry location was a priority.

It just wasn't possible at the moment.

The river wound around a bend. Another rapid came into view. Sophie clenched her teeth as Aiden bellowed out instructions. They were nearly out of the rapid when they bounced off a boulder that was half-buried in the river. The force of the collision dumped Levi out of the craft. Celine and Sophie cried out.

"Levi!" Aiden lurched forward and grabbed at his friend. He yanked and tugged. Sophie and Celine helped as much as they could. He was nearly inside when they crashed into another boulder. With horror, she watched as Aiden's back slammed into it and his head brushed against it. She and Celine got him back into the raft.

"We have to get out of the river," he mumbled, his voice slurred. He was losing consciousness and attempted to shake it off, grimacing. When he heaved himself back to where he had been and took up her oar, she opened her mouth. Although what she planned to say was a mystery. She just knew he was in bad shape.

"Don't argue," he told her. "I have to keep going. Once we make it to the bank, we still have to find a way to get Levi warm."

"You, too." He might imagine himself invincible, she thought as she scanned him for signs of shock, but he wasn't.

Levi was still bleeding. She pulled off her cardigan. It was sopping wet but better than nothing. Tossing it to Celine, she signed, "Fold this up and hold it against his shoulder. Keep pressure on it."

Celine's mouth formed an *O*. "I don't want to hurt him!"

"We need to stop the bleeding to keep him alive."

Gingerly she did as she was told. Sophie's heart stirred in empathy as she watched her little sister caring for Levi. Levi was so much like her brother had been. His attitude toward her sister made her wonder if he had siblings of his own that he had cared for. Briefly, she wondered why he was estranged from his family.

After roughly fifteen minutes of struggling against the current, the raft hit the bank with a hard bounce. Aiden grunted. Sophie winced in sympathy. It took them the better part of half an hour, but together, Aiden, Sophie and Celine were able to carry Levi over the bank and up to street level. They halted in a patch of sunlight near a dirt-and-gravel road. No cars were in sight as far as she could see.

That was both good and bad. Good because those who wanted to kill them weren't running at them. Bad because Levi needed help. So did Aiden.

"We can't stay here near the road. Let's go into the field across the road. It's sunny, but if we sit in the tall grass, no one will see us from the road," Aiden said.

Sweat was pouring down her back by the time they'd set Levi down in the grass. She wiped off her face with her arm.

"Where do you think we are?"

Aiden didn't answer. "Aiden?"

Her heart was in her throat as she spun around, searching for him.

He was sitting a few feet away with his back braced against a tree.

"Sophie," he rumbled out, barely audible.

She ran to his side and knelt down.

"I'm here. What can I do for you?" Reaching out, she placed the back of her hand against his forehead. It was clammy. That was definitely not good.

Why was he smiling?

She removed her hand. To her surprise, he grabbed it in his and held on. "We'll be okay. Pray."

When he slumped over, tears distorted her vision. She brushed them away on her sleeve. Crying wouldn't help anyone. Leaning over, she placed her fingers on his neck. The pulse nearly brought on a second bout of tears.

Pushing herself to her feet, she crossed over to where Levi lay. She didn't know what else she could do for him. Everything they had was wet.

In a rush, she opened the backpack and pulled out Celine's processors. She'd placed them in a Ziploc bag. The baggie was damp, but the devices appeared to be dry.

She handed them over to Celine. "They'll need to be recharged soon. We don't have the charger with us."

"Will Aiden and Levi die?"

Sophie dropped down next to her sister and looped her arm around the child. Her heart ached for her. The fact that she didn't know how to make everything better gnawed at her. She wasn't used to feeling helpless. "I won't lie to you. I'm really worried about Levi. I think Aiden just needs some rest."

"He likes you. Aiden does. At least I think he does."

What? Where had that come from? Her cheeks heated as her sister turned her head to observe her. Celine was trying to distract herself. She hoped.

"He doesn't like me," Sophie signed without her voice, just in case he was conscious enough to hear her. She felt like she was in junior high having a conversation about boys. "He's helping us. That's all."

"Uh-huh."

Celine might have said more, but Sophie shushed her. "Hold on. I hear something coming."

It wasn't a sound she heard much in Chicago, but she'd know it anywhere. It was the steady clip-clop of horse hooves. A single horse, if her guess was correct. She needed to see who was coming. Her shoulders tightened as the list of possibilities ran through her mind. Surely, the men who were after them would not be on horseback.

Rising up on her knees, Sophie slowly lifted her head above the tall grass. Just high enough so she had a view of what was coming. That way, if it was someone who could help them, she could stand up and wave him down. Otherwise, she was fairly confident that she could drop down again and hide.

At least she pretended she was feeling confident. For Celine's sake.

Initially she couldn't see anyone, though the clip-clop of hooves continued to get closer. Now she could hear another sound. Some sort of motorless vehicle.

Finally, the horse cleared the trees. It was pulling a buggy, driven by an Amish man around her father's age.

What should she do? She didn't want to involve a stranger, but the men needed care. The Amish would not take them to the police, nor was it likely they had seen their pictures on the television. Levi had said his family was Amish. Should she relate that to the man? Or was that something she shouldn't mention?

Decided, she realized that the man had started to drive past.

If she was going to get help, she needed to act fast.

TEN

Jumping to her feet, Sophie ran toward the road, waving her hands to get the man's attention.

"Hey!"

Startled, the Amish man pulled on the reins he was holding. The horse trotted a couple horse lengths before coming to a halt. Sophie no longer felt the pain in her legs as desperation had her running out to where he was stopped in the middle of the dirt road.

"Hey," she panted as she reached the buggy.

She stopped to get her breath, wondering what she could tell him.

"Are you in trouble?" the man asked her.

She blinked rapidly. "Yes. I am. I'm with my sister and two of our friends over there." She pointed in the direction of where she'd left her companions. Suddenly she realized that she could tell the man part of the truth.

"We went rafting, and my friends were injured. Both of them are unconscious."

His eyebrows winged upward, hiding beneath his light brown bangs.

"*Ach*! Show me where."

He followed her to where Celine waited with the men. Levi's breathing was harsh. His color was awful. Aiden was in the same condition he'd been in previously. The Amish man bent closer to Levi, removing the cardigan that had been used to stem the blood.

"This man's been shot." He stood and faced Sophie.

"Yes." She sucked in a breath to fortify herself. She'd tell him as much as she could. It was the only decent thing to do. If he decided to help them, it would put him at peril. He deserved to make that choice with full knowledge of what he was choosing.

She hoped that he didn't decide to take his horse and buggy and return home.

"He was shot helping us. That man—" she pointed to Aiden "—is a cop. He was hurt rescuing my sister and myself from men who want to hurt us. He was injured when they came after us. I'm afraid that if I don't get them help fast, they'll die."

At her words, Celine buried her face in her hands.

"You should get them to a hospital, ain't so? I can drive you to town and you can call an ambulance."

Okay, this was where it could get tricky. She needed his help, and she had to do whatever she could to convince him.

"Sir, we can't go to the hospital. Or to the police. They think we killed someone."

His face went blank. He wasn't going to help. She'd tried to convince him, but it was no use.

"We didn't kill anyone," she hurried to explain. She probably shouldn't have said that, except she felt that she should be honest with this man. It wouldn't be fair to give him less than the truth. She tried again. "Please, sir, Aiden didn't kill anyone. He was framed."

He stilled. "Aiden who?"

"Forster. Aiden Forster."

"I know of him."

She stared at him, shocked. What were the chances that the person who came by would know of Aiden? She'd say it was a coincidence, but she didn't believe that. Once again, God was showing His care for them. She was humbled. And a little bit awed.

"Really? You know him?" She pointed back at Aiden.

The man gave her a small smile and shook his head slightly. "*Nee*. I don't know him. I know of him."

She waited. After a few seconds, it was apparent that he had told her all he was planning to say. Hopefully, whatever he knew about Aiden would be enough to convince him to assist them.

She grabbed on to her courage. "If you know of him, then you know that he is a man of honor. Someone who takes his duty to protect and serve seriously." She gestured to Levi. "This young man will die if he doesn't get help soon."

He pulled on his beard while he thought. Finally, he appeared to come to a decision and nodded his head.

"*Ja*. I will help you. I will need my son. Wait here. I will be back."

He climbed back up in his buggy and picked up the reins. "My *haus* is down the road. I will return in ten minutes."

He clicked his teeth and flicked the reins. The horse

started off at a steady trot. Sophie watched until the buggy was out of sight. She had no idea how long she stood there waiting until the low hum of a motor coming closer sent her running back to where the others were hiding. She sat down beside her sister and was out of sight before the vehicle passed.

"Will he help us?" Celine asked.

"Yes, he's gone to get someone else."

They waited in silence. The time dragged on. Hadn't it been ten minutes yet? Maybe he'd changed his mind. Or maybe he had really gone to the police.

Anxiety crawled like ants through her. Even her skin itched with it. The need to move had her rocking in place as she sat. Shifting restlessly, Sophie tried to decide what else they could do.

Nothing. There was nothing else she could do. There was no way she and Celine would be able to carry two men who were unconscious. And there was definitely not a chance that she would abandon them. Nor was she comfortable with the idea of leaving them to go find help.

You can pray.

She could pray. She could give the whole situation to God and allow Him to take control. Wasn't that what she had said she was going to do from now on? It was hard. She had been in control of her own life for so long that the thought of letting go was an uncomfortable sensation. It made her feel a little twitchy to not be in charge of what was happening.

She scoffed at herself. When was the last time she had really been in charge? Yeah, sure, she lived by herself. She was making career decisions. But her personal life she had no control over. If she'd had control of what happened in her life, her parents and Brian would still be alive, and Celine would not be in this danger. Nor would she.

Closing her eyes, she bowed her head. "God, I can't control this situation. I have no idea what I'm doing or what will happen. Please take over. Calm my anxiety and bring help. And please let these men recover."

Peace washed over her. Oh, she was still scared and concerned for their safety. But she wasn't alone. That knowledge was finally sinking in deep.

The staccato drum of hooves on the road brought her head up. She didn't want to raise her hopes. No doubt there were many Amish families living in this part of the country. She wasn't even sure if they were in Pennsylvania or Ohio. Tilting her head, she listened critically. The noise was coming from the direction in which the man had driven away.

The noise stopped. She heard boots hit the ground. More than one person.

Her heartbeat increased.

Now they would discover if the man had truly brought help or simply turned them in.

Several male voices drifted over to where they were hiding.

"Dat, are you sure this is where you left them?"

"*Ja*, they are here somewhere."

She recognized the second male. It was the man she'd talked to. Cautious, she rose so her eyes were above the grass. There were two men, both in Amish dress. One was younger, late teens maybe. His face was clean-shaven, so she knew he was unmarried. The horse was no longer pulling a buggy. Now she saw it hitched to some kind of flatbed trailer.

So that's what had taken them so long.

She nearly wilted with relief. They were truly going to assist them even though they were strangers.

"There you are." They moved to where she was hiding. The man pointed at Aiden. "Does he look familiar?"

His son strode closer to Aiden. "*Ja*. I'm not sure. It was two years ago, but this might have been him."

Might have been him what? She was hoping one of them would enlighten her; instead, they went to Levi and began to move him to the trailer.

"Easy, now. We don't want to hurt the man. Watch your step." The father kept up a steady stream of comments as they carried first Levi, then Aiden, to the trailer. When they were done, he walked over to where Sophie and Celine stood.

"It would be best if you rode in back with them."

His accent was thicker than Levi's. Celine looked at her, not sure what to do. Sophie understood. Celine was so exhausted that she was finding it difficult to read lips. Well, she could ease some of the strain for the girl. She signed the instructions to her sister. Neither man reacted to the obvious clue that she was deaf.

Celine asked a question.

"My sister wants to know your names."

"*Ach*! Of course she does. I'm Silas King, and this is my son, Melvin."

Within minutes, they were settled into the trailer and on their way to the King home. Sophie's whole body ached. She was tired, mentally and physically, and was ready to fall asleep on her feet. It had been hours since they'd eaten, but she was past feeling hungry.

She heard sirens coming toward them from the other direction. Motioning her sister to stay low, she hunkered down next to Aiden. When an emergency vehicle zoomed past, she let out the breath she'd been holding but didn't straighten up. She remained in that position until Silas pulled the trailer into his driveway.

As Silas and Melvin carried Levi into the house, Aiden stirred.

"Sophie?"

"Shh. It's fine." She leaned down and kissed his forehead. Celine snickered. Sophie ignored her sister the best she could. What had come over her, kissing him?

"Sophie, are you hurt?"

Aiden's eyes blinked open for a moment.

"No."

She would have said more if he had not grimaced and closed his eyes again. They could talk when he was awake.

All that mattered at the moment was that they were safe.

For now.

Where was he?

Aiden blinked at the bright morning light coming through a window. He was in a strange room, in a strange bed and wearing someone else's clothes. The walls were a warm off-white shade, and there were no pictures on them. The furnishings were simple. A dresser, a chest, a bed. No lamps. No light switches.

It wasn't a room he'd ever been in, but it was comfortable. The warmth of the bed called to him. He was still so drained it would be wonderful to close his eyes and sink back into sleep.

His lids drifted shut. His mind began to clear. He had a vague recollection of talking to Sophie while riding in some kind of trailer or buggy.

Sophie! And Celine. Were they here? Were they safe? And then there was Levi. The last he knew, Levi had been shot and had lost blood. Where was Levi?

He couldn't stay in this room, all warm and cozy, while they could be in danger. Or worse. The image of Phillip catching up and taking the girls while leaving Aiden for dead flashed through his mind.

Completely awake now, he flung off the covers and swung his feet over the edge of the bed to sit up. Immediately, his head protested. He dropped his head in his hands and sat for a moment while the room whirled around him.

He'd been so worried about the others he hadn't taken inventory of his own physical issues. Vaguely, he recalled hitting his head on a rock.

When he was sure he could stand without falling down, he pushed himself slowly to his feet and lifted his head. The room didn't spin, which was a good sign. Nothing seemed broken, although he felt like one big bruise. He could deal with that. He was alive. He took a quick look around the room, searching for his boots.

When he didn't find them, he had to resign himself to walking around in socks. Not his first choice, though, again, he'd manage. He did, however, find one of the phones they'd purchased. He looked at it. It had only eighteen percent battery. He needed to call his chief before it was too late. He shoved it in his pocket. Now to find Sophie and the others.

Leaving the quiet confines of the bedroom, he moved out into the hall. He was on the first floor, which made sense. Whoever had brought him here probably wouldn't have wanted to carry his deadweight up a flight of stairs.

His musings again reminded him of Levi. The sense of urgency increased. He made his way down the hall. It opened up into a large open room. Again, the furnishings were very simple. Hardwood floors and no family pictures on the walls.

There was a large cast-iron stove, the type mostly used for burning wood to heat homes, near the far end of the room.

He realized that he was in an Amish home. The question was—whose? He doubted that they had made it to Levi's family home. They hadn't traveled far enough down the river. Surely he hadn't been unconscious for that long?

A door opened and shut in the next room, and he heard the soft hum of voices. They were not speaking English, and he couldn't make out what they were saying.

It was time to meet the owner of the house.

Stepping around the corner, Aiden came face-to-face

with an older man pouring himself a cup of coffee from a silver kettle on the stove. A woman stood at the counter, mixing something in a large bowl.

"Gut," the man grunted. "You are awake."

The man set down his coffee and introduced himself. "I'm Silas King. This is my wife, Eleanor."

He nodded at them and shook the man's hand.

"Aiden Forster. I want to thank you for your trouble."

Silas waved away his thanks and picked up his coffee. "It was no trouble. Would you like some coffee? Breakfast? Your friends have been worried about you."

Breakfast and coffee sounded wonderful, after he made sure everyone else was safe. "My friends—are they all right? All of them."

"Ja. They are well. Celine and Sophie are out in the barn with my daughter, Mary. Your friend Levi, the one who was shot, he is still sleeping. We had a doctor over to see him last night."

Some of Aiden's alarm must have shown on his face, for the man stepped closer and held out his hands in a calming manner. "Now don't be getting anxious. The doctor, he is a *gut* man. He will take care of your friend. He is also a man who understands how to keep a secret, so he will not be calling the police."

"How can he not call the police? Isn't that part of his obligation? To report gunshot wounds and anything that looks like criminal behavior?"

"Ja, maybe so. If he was treating patients in an *Englisch* hospital. Not in a Plain home."

His muscles relaxed. "Did he ask you what happened?"

"*Ja*, he asked."

Aiden waited. "And? What did you tell him?"

Silas chuckled, his eyes gleaming with mischief. "I did not tell him anything. Your Sophie explained it. You'll have to ask her about it."

Aiden's ears grew uncomfortably warm, hearing the words "your Sophie." Why would the man assume that they were together? Other than the fact that they had been traveling together. Had Sophie said something?

He would have to wait until he had talked with Sophie. In the meantime, as much as he wanted to rush out and make sure that she and her sister were all right, it seemed clear to him that Levi had to take precedence. If he looked at him now, he could see for himself whether his friend was going to be fine where he was or if he actually needed to take him to the hospital. Levi would hate going to the hospital, but Aiden knew he would if it was necessary.

"Would it be possible for me to see Levi now?" he questioned his host politely.

Five minutes later, he was looking down at Levi. He rubbed his neck, knowing in his heart that it was his fault Levi was in this mess. While he wasn't sure what else he could have done, if he hadn't shown up at Levi's house, his friend would not have been shot.

But he had been.

Enough!

He couldn't change the past. He had made decisions based on the urgency of the situation. If he had to do it all again, he might make the same decision. Because even though Levi had been shot, if he hadn't made that decision then the Larson sisters might very well be dead right now.

Still, he couldn't quite get past the guilt of failing someone else and allowing a friend to be injured.

Levi stirred and opened his eyes. He seemed confused at first, and then his gaze cleared as he focused on Aiden. "Hey. Where are we?"

As Aiden explained their current situation, Levi listened intently. "And the girls?"

"I haven't seen them yet." He hesitated. "Look, I'm sorry I—"

"*Ach.* Don't apologize. You did what you had to do. I would have done the same. Do me a favor, though. Go check on the girls. I think we'll both feel better after you see them."

Aiden didn't need to be told twice. He said he'd see Levi later and followed Silas's directions out to the barn.

As he neared, a familiar laugh cut right through him and nearly stopped his heart. For just a moment, he leaned against the outside wall, gathering his strength and composing himself before he went in. Once he was sure he wouldn't disgrace himself, he straightened up and entered the barn.

He passed a clothesline and saw that all of their clothes were hanging out to dry. He smiled, wondering if his girls looked like Amish girls now.

Not his girls. He had to remember that. Otherwise, it would be difficult to leave when this was over.

And he had to leave. There were things he had to accomplish that he couldn't focus on while he was in charge of anyone's safety.

Even thinking about saying farewell left him hollow.

Sophie and Celine were standing next to a young Amish girl. Sure enough, they were both wearing long dresses. Celine's was a lovely light blue. Sophie's—

She took his breath away. The jade green dress brought out the fire in her hair. From where he stood, he had a clear view of her face. Seeing the smile on her face released a spark of joy inside him. One he wasn't sure he'd ever felt before.

She turned to find him watching, and her smile widened into a full grin. "Aiden!"

She flew at him. He barely had time to open his arms before she leaped into them and squeezed him, hard.

He didn't mind at all. Having her in his arms felt natural, like she belonged there. He was reluctant to let her go. When she loosened her grip, though, he did the same.

Her face was bright pink when she backed away. "Oops." A nervous laugh spilled from her lips. "I didn't mean to do that. It's just that we've been worried about you."

"It's fine. I didn't mind. I was concerned about you, as well."

He couldn't be pulled in by the attraction simmering between them, yet he found it difficult to distance himself.

The spell was broken by the phone ringing. He startled, then shook his head. He didn't even need to look at the number to know who was calling.

"Yes, Brad?"

"Hey, I hate to keep calling you, but I thought you

should know that someone has reported Levi missing. You are suspected in his kidnapping."

"I'm what?" This was unbelievable.

"Sorry, Aiden. I thought you should know."

"I appreciate it, Brad."

He hung up the phone, his mind whirling.

It felt like a net was slowly closing in around him. And around those he was trying so hard to protect.

ELEVEN

She couldn't believe that she had jumped into his arms like that! Sophie was mortified.

Until she saw the look on his face as he talked to Brad on the phone. He had moved away from her so that he could talk privately, which was ridiculous since she had every right to know what was going on.

Since she was watching him, she noticed the instant his jaw clenched tight and his face went blank.

Whatever it was, it wasn't good.

When he hung up, he casually asked her if she wanted to go for a walk. He cast a significant glance at Celine. Sophie got the message. He wanted to relay what Brad had said to her privately.

Tapping Celine's shoulder to get her attention, she informed her that they'd be outside the barn. Celine was more interested in the animals that Mary was showing her. In fact, she could barely take her eyes off the new baby calf long enough to watch her sister sign. No sooner had Sophie finished than Celine was waving her away and turning her back.

Sophie grinned. Her sister would be just fine.

"I think I've been replaced," she joked to Aiden. His lips twitched upward in a crooked half smile, but she could see that his heart wasn't in it. The smile vanished as quickly as it had come.

Apparently without thought, Aiden took her hand to tug her along in his quest to find a quiet spot to talk. She liked the feel of her hand in his. She liked it far too much. She knew they had no future. Aiden obviously had some things in his past that he hadn't shared with her, and she had to focus on her sister.

It didn't stop her from wishing things were different, though.

When they were far enough away from the barn he finally spoke.

"You probably heard that that was Brad on the phone."

She nodded and tugged her hand from his in order to wrap both arms around herself to ward off the sudden chill. Brad had called them three times so far, and it had always been bad news. Although, without his calls, they would probably have been caught by now. So it was good that he gave them a heads-up. She was just so tired of running.

She hunched slightly as her stomach clenched.

He didn't keep her waiting long.

He reached out and rubbed his hand up her arm. He probably wasn't even aware that he did it. For some reason, he seemed to need to touch her when he was giving her bad news. She wouldn't complain, as she found comfort in his touch.

"Apparently somebody reported Levi missing. My guess is the police found our phones and have connected us to Levi."

She thought about this new piece of information for a minute.

"Well, I don't think we're any worse off than we were before. I mean, they're already looking for you and me."

"I know, but I'm wondering who reported him missing. Levi doesn't get very many visitors. I'm inclined to think that it might have come from Phillip. His men followed us to Levi's place. So he obviously knows that we were with Levi, at least at one point. So now the police will be looking for him, as well."

She frowned, pondering the situation. "Will he get in any hot water? For helping us?"

Aiden shrugged and looked off in the distance. "I don't know. He might. There are several charges they can throw at him. I don't know, Soph. I think we need to leave him here and continue. Let's go talk with him."

They wandered inside the house. Melvin and Silas were both gone. "They work at the lumber mill a mile up the road," Eleanor said with a smile. She had two smaller children with her. One, in a high chair with a bowl of cereal, was eating. The other, a small girl, hid behind her mother's skirts.

A twinge of guilt poked her. This nice family didn't deserve to be involved in this mess.

Eleanor looked at the clock. "The older children won't be home yet for two hours. They are helping their *grossmamma* bake pies today. Supper will be at four."

"Thank you. We're just going to visit our friend Levi for a bit."

Eleanor looked scandalized. "You can't go in his room!"

Sophie blinked at her. "We'll leave the door open. But we have to talk with him."

Although Eleanor didn't look happy about it, she didn't argue. Sophie hated making an issue of it, especially as they were guests in their home, but she refused to be left out of a discussion that could impact her or Celine.

A few minutes later, they were talking to Levi.

"*Ja*, I think we should leave for my family's old community."

He tried to sit up and blanched. Aiden was there, pushing him back down.

"No, not this time. You need a little time to recoup."

Sophie looked at Aiden. "Maybe in a day or so?"

"We'll see."

They left Levi and headed back outside. Together they meandered into the barn to see how Celine was getting on. She was showing her new friend some signs. They seemed to be doing well, so Aiden and Sophie decided not to bother them.

Leaving the barn, Sophie inhaled deeply. She loved the scent of honeysuckle that was heavy in the air. It reminded her of home.

"You amaze me, you know that?"

Surprised, she jerked her head to look at Aiden. "Me? Why would you say that?"

She couldn't think of anything amazing she'd done,

ever; neither could she deny the admiration she saw in his eyes.

"Look at you," he said, waving his hand at her. "You've suffered a tremendous loss, your uncle is trying to kill you, I nearly drowned you in a raft when you have a fear of water, and here you are, smiling and talking with me like nothing is wrong. Like I said. Amazing."

Her face grew warm with his praise, and she grinned at him. "I guess I am kind of amazing, huh?" She grew serious. "I don't have a choice. I have Celine to look after. And in spite of almost drowning me," she said, using her fingers to make air quotes, "you have been the one keeping us alive. I won't forget all that you have done for us."

His mouth twisted in not really a grimace yet not a smile.

"What? Aiden, what is it that haunts you?"

He kicked at a pebble with his boot. She thought he wouldn't answer, and then he shrugged.

"I have a sister. Jennie. She was the sweetest thing. I think of her when I look at Celine."

She'd wondered if Celine reminded him of someone. Her heart was already pounding. Even though he'd used the present tense, letting her know Jennie was still alive, she had a hunch this story did not have a happy ending.

"What happened?"

"Our dad died when we were young. I looked out for Jennie while our mom worked. She worked a lot to pay the bills. Every night, she'd tell me to look out for Jennie. So I did." He reached down and picked up a rock.

She watched him toss it from hand to hand, waiting until he was ready to continue. "When I was thirteen, my mother married again. Jennie, she was only nine. I'm not even sure how mom met Steve. He was just there in our lives, always bringing gifts and saying nice things. I didn't trust him. Kids know when someone is not telling the truth. But Mom married him."

They were at the house. He sat down on a step and patted the space beside him. She sank onto the sun-warmed wooden stair.

"It took all of two weeks before he showed his true colors. At first, he'd just yell. When he was drunk, Mom would make excuses. We learned to stay out of his way. When Jennie was eleven, Steve went after her. I locked the two of us in my bedroom and called the cops. I thought that would solve everything. He'd go to jail and we'd be alone with Mom again."

She put her head against his shoulder, longing to comfort him. When she felt him kiss the top of her head, she closed her eyes to keep the tears from streaking down her cheeks.

"That didn't happen, I take it."

"Nope. Oh, Steve went to jail, all right. But Mom? Well, the system decided that she was unfit. They put both Jennie and I in foster care. Separately. When we were both older, I tried to find her. She wanted nothing to do with me. I'd failed her, you see. She blamed me for the fact that she was in foster care."

She sat up fast. "Wait a minute, she blamed you? That was not your fault."

He wouldn't meet her eyes.

"Aiden. Aiden, look at me."

Finally, he tilted his head so she could see his face. "Please don't tell me that you are holding yourself responsible. You were a kid. A kid who should not have had that burden in the first place. And Steve deserved to be in jail."

This time when he smiled, she could see that it warmed his eyes. "I know that. In my mind, I understand. In my heart, I still feel like I failed her. And she hasn't talked to me since."

"Don't give up on her. She might come around. Sometimes we need to grow up to see the truth."

He had never told anyone about what had happened to him and Jennie. Not his partner. Not Levi. No one.

He'd almost backed out of telling Sophie. The urge to tell was a pressure building inside him. At that moment, he'd had to tell her. The confession left him feeling strangely weightless. As if the burden he'd carried had been made of bricks that were weighing him down.

He glanced her direction. Her lovely hazel gaze caught him and drew him in.

In that instant, he knew he was going to kiss her. Was it a bad idea? Absolutely. Still, he couldn't find the strength to pull away. He should crack a joke or make some lighthearted remark to break the mood.

He didn't.

Instead, he found himself leaning closer to her. He moved slowly, giving her time to retreat, but she seemed to be as stuck as he was.

Her lids fluttered closed. He could feel her breath on his face.

Tires rumbling up the driveway brought him to his senses. No, he couldn't kiss her. That wouldn't be fair. He pulled away from her, but that wasn't enough. He needed to put some distance between them. Abruptly he stood and walked away from her. After a few steps, he couldn't resist and glanced back at her over his shoulder.

Sophie's face was red. She shifted and stood, brushing imaginary dust from her dress. He hadn't meant to embarrass her. Then he saw the flash of her eyes. Nope. She wasn't embarrassed. His Sophie was mad.

He kept the grin that wanted to break free locked up tight, but it was a struggle. Why she made him so happy was something he wasn't prepared to analyze. And seeing her mad that he had broken off their almost-kiss, well, it made him want to laugh. Not in mockery. Never that. He was just happy to know that she'd wanted the kiss as much as he did.

Which was absolutely not a good idea.

Especially since they had someone out to kill them. He had to remember that. Whatever he was feeling, no matter how pleasant, needed to take a back seat to keeping her safe and nailing Phillip Larson.

It made no sense to dwell on it. He pivoted on his heel and watched an old maroon sedan driving slowly up the driveway. He could walk faster than the car was crawling along. However, since this was a residence and young children lived here, he approved. If only more people were as cautious when they drove.

"Oh, that's the doctor," Sophie said, coming to his

side. "He was here last night and gave you a fairly clean bill of health. Except for the head. You gotta watch that."

Aiden nodded. His instinct to flee remained, but the doctor had already seen them. He wanted to determine what kind of threat the man posed for them.

First, they had to wait for the doctor to park his car. The man pulled up, then did a six-point turn to get the vehicle facing the other direction. It would make it easier when it was time to leave, but it was amusing to watch.

"I could do that with only three points," he murmured, winking when she rolled her eyes at him.

"Bragging?"

He liked this banter. He knew what they were really doing, defusing some of the tension.

At last the doctor turned off his engine and stepped from the vehicle. He looked to be in his late sixties and walked with a decided limp. His face, while kind, had a somber expression.

"Well, son, you seem to be feeling better than the last time I saw you." The man ran a clinical gaze over him, stopping to visually analyze the bruising on his temple. "How's the head treating you?"

"Not too bad. Nothing I can't handle."

"Huh. I bet you would say that even if it was hurting like Silas's mule had kicked you."

Beside him, Sophie snickered. Clearly, she agreed with the doctor's assessment. He wasn't sure he appreciated their views.

"Come on, Aiden," she said, nudging him with her elbow. "Smile. It's true and you know it."

Okay, yeah, maybe they were correct.

A rusty chuckle left the doctor. He started to move up the stairs at a painful pace. When Aiden moved to assist him, he brushed him away. "Don't you worry about me. I've got a few years of stair climbing ahead of me before I retire." The doctor stayed for about an hour. Fifteen minutes to check on Levi, and another forty-five to chat with Silas after he arrived home.

When they went in to eat, it was a dining experience like he'd never had. Eleanor and Silas had six children. Melvin was the oldest. Next in line was Mary, a shy girl around Celine's age. Then there was a set of identical twin boys that Aiden couldn't tell apart. An adorable three-year-old named Laura sat in wooden booster chair next to her mother. On the other side of Eleanor was a high chair with the baby of the family buckled in it. All the food was on the table, including a water pitcher. Before they started to eat, everyone bowed their heads and prayed silently. They stayed bowed until Silas said, "Amen."

No one fussed about eating their vegetables. Not even the youngest children. And they all ate everything on their plates. He shook his head.

"Something wrong, Aiden?" Melvin inquired as he helped himself to a second helping of chicken.

"I've never seen children eat their veggies so well."

Eleanor smiled, practically preening. *"Danke."*

When dessert was passed around, Aiden was so full he had to pass. And tired. It had been an exhausting few days, and now all he wanted was to crash.

But he was restless, and after dinner was done, he

stepped outside. It wasn't quite dark yet, but the light was starting to dim. He heard the door close and knew immediately who it was.

"Hey. This is like déjà vu."

He smiled at the laughter bubbling in her voice. His smile faded as he considered all that had happened since that early morning on the porch with her.

"Will life ever go back to normal, do you think?" Her words were so soft he leaned in to catch them.

"Yes and no." He leaned a shoulder against one of the pillars on the porch and moved so he could watch her. "You'll go back to your old life. But you've been through some things that will never leave you. So you will be different."

Wow. He didn't know he could be so profound. Must be the tiredness.

"I know one thing that's changed." She tilted her head. Her eyes gleamed in the fading light. "I have begun to rearrange my priorities. God, family and career. Before, I had put career first. I will always regret not appreciating my parents while they were here."

He could relate to that.

She shifted closer. His traitorous mind flashed back to when he had nearly kissed her. It was fortunate the doctor had shown up although, truth be told, Aiden regretted not kissing her as much as he would have regretted it if they had kissed.

Completely ridiculous.

"Have you talked with your chief yet?"

"Huh?" Sophie's voice dragged him away from his thoughts. "Oh, no. Not yet. Let me do that now."

He pulled the cell phone that he'd been carrying out of his pocket. Only seven percent of the battery was left. He hoped it was enough. He dialed the chief's personal number.

She picked up on the first ring. "Wanda Daniels."

"It's me. Aiden."

"Aiden, where are you?" she whispered urgently into the phone. "Do you know that you are wanted for questioning?"

Wincing, he pinched the bridge of his eyes. "Yes, I'm aware. The kid who was killed, he was the one that Larson was talking with when Sophie walked in on them. He had disappointed Larson, lost him a deal."

"I figured it was something like that. You still have the two Larson girls?"

"Yes, ma'am. They're fine."

"Where are you?" she asked again.

He paused, unwilling to give away too much. "Are you sure this phone is safe?"

"Yes. I had this phone and my office swept for bugs last night. We're good. Are you going to answer my question?"

He knew that tone. She was done taking excuses and expected immediate compliance.

"Yes, ma'am. We're in Ohio. Near Berlin. Hang on," he said when Sophie waved at him.

Covering the phone microphone with his hand, he looked at her.

She glanced at the phone in his hand. "I talked with Silas this morning," she whispered to him. "We're in

Fisher Village, a New Order Amish community. We're only an hour outside of Berlin."

He nodded and relayed the information to his chief. "Have you found the mole yet?"

There was some shifting on the other end. "Wait a sec. Berlin. Okay, I see it on the map. That's Amish country. You converting, Forster?"

He laughed. "No. But my buddy Levi has family there. We're going to see if we can stay there."

"Gotcha. As to your mole question, we have Officer Quail under watch."

"I don't believe it."

Quail was as solid as they came. He was young, but everything about him read *cop*. He was completely by the book. Even though he was a bit of a rookie, he was loyal to a fault. There was no way it was him.

"I thought the same thing. But we have to follow the evidence. And right now, it's pointing to him."

Well, it could point to him all it wanted to. He wouldn't believe it until he had a chance to look at the supposed evidence himself.

TWELVE

"Levi explained to us what's been going on."

Silas had caught Aiden right after breakfast. On his guard, Aiden quirked an eyebrow at Silas.

"Oh? What did he tell you?"

"Most of it we knew. You are a police officer. Celine and Sophie are being chased by their uncle." Silas took his hat off a hook and gestured for Aiden to walk with him. The men stepped outside. It was a cool morning that smelled like rain was coming.

"All that is true," Aiden said. "Levi was leading us to his family's place. I guess they live right in Berlin."

"*Ja*, so he told me." The older man tugged on his beard. "I'm thinking that if you still plan to go there, Levi won't be going with you."

Unfortunately, the doctor had declared that Levi's wound was infected, and he needed to remain exactly where he was in order for it to be treated. Which meant either they remain as well or go on without him.

Aiden was itching to be on his way. He felt they were too close to where they had started.

Frustrated, he blew out a breath, hard.

"I don't mean to sound ungrateful, because I am grateful, but I believe that me and the girls should keep going. I'd hate to bring harm to your family."

"Kind of you. But Gott will keep us safe. It's all in His hands." He took a sip of his coffee. "If you need something to do, we could use a hand."

"Thanks for the offer, but I think it would be better if no one knew we were here."

"*Ja*. The doctor knows."

Was that a warning?

"Is he likely to talk?"

"*Nee*. Edward is a *gut* friend. He won't talk. Unless—"

"Unless what?" he barked, then grimaced. Rubbing his hand over his face, he apologized. "Don't pay any mind to me. I'm a little tense these days."

To his relief, Silas chuckled, his eyes twinkling. "*Ja*. This I can see. You are a man protecting his own. I understand."

Well, not exactly. But he did feel like Celine and Sophie were his responsibility, so he didn't correct the man. *Admit it. You like the idea of them being yours. And you belonging to them.* He did like it. He just wouldn't act on those feelings.

"*Cumme*, the other men at the mill are all Amish. If I say you are a *gut* man and not a threat, they will take my word."

Aiden opened his mouth to refuse politely, then stopped. He would like to scope out the area a bit. What better way to gauge if his enemies had found them? If these men could be trusted not to go to the police, would he be able to casually inquire if anyone had heard anything or seen any strangers about town?

"Maybe…" He looked at his clothes. He had put on his old jeans out of habit that morning. "I don't know if it would be a problem, but I stand out in my own clothes."

"Ja." The man frowned at his attire. "I suppose you could dress in Plain clothes for a few days. You and Melvin are around the same size. He isn't as tall as you, though."

There was enough hesitation in the man's words to make Aiden wonder if he'd be asking him to break some sort of taboo.

"If it would get you in trouble—"

"Nee, it would be safer for you." He shrugged. "Eleanor already found clothes for Celine and Sophie, and they can wear them again. Finding clothes for you won't matter."

Aiden nodded. "It would also be safer for your family not to have three non-Amish people walking around your house."

Within an hour, Aiden, Sophie and Celine were all fully dressed in Amish clothes. The women were wearing the same dresses they'd put on the day before while their clothes were washed. Aiden loved that shade of green on Sophie. It was difficult to not stare at her. Man, she was pretty. But it went deeper than that. She was spunky and brave and kind.

There were no buttons on the dresses. Eleanor had shown Sophie how to braid their hair and pin it up before donning the starched white prayer *kapp*. The moment he saw the *kapp* on Sophie's head, he smiled at the picture she made. At the same time, he missed seeing her gorgeous hair. When Celine went to tie the strings, Eleanor stopped her with a gentle hand.

"*Nee*. We leave the *kapp* strings untied." Sophie signed the comments for her sister's benefit.

Celine shrugged and allowed the strings to drop. When she left the house for the barn, he frowned. She was stomping a bit more than usual. He caught Sophie's attention when she sighed.

"What's going on with Celine?"

"She's frustrated at not hearing."

"Because we're in disguise."

She lifted her hands. He could see the frustration shimmering in her eyes, too. "Her processors need to be charged, and there is no electricity here. And when we left the car, we left her charging port in it. So we are going to be dealing with a cranky preteen until I can get a new charger."

Which could be a while.

He didn't envy Sophie the task of dealing with her sister. He'd help as much as he could, but at the end of the day, she was the one handling most of the drama.

"Look, I'm going with Silas to the mill today. I'm going to ask around and see if anyone has seen or heard anything."

"Wouldn't it be more beneficial to ask around in the nearest town?"

"Maybe. But we can't take the risk of being identified. Also, I don't know who we could trust not to repeat what we say. Either way, this might be our safest choice."

She didn't look happy about it, but she nodded. "Celine and I promised to help Eleanor with her chores today, although I doubt Celine will be much help. She's been in a mood all morning."

Reaching out, he caught and squeezed her hand. "Hey, she might surprise you."

She squeezed back before removing her hand from his. "We'll see."

When Silas announced it was time to go, Aiden grabbed the straw hat he'd been loaned off the peg near the back door and followed the older man out to the buggy. Heaving himself up on the seat, he settled in next to Silas.

He wasn't used to riding in a buggy, and it was obvious. Sitting up on the bench with Silas, he kept his hands planted firmly on the bench on either side of himself to keep his balance. When the horse first started, the buggy jolted forward. Aiden fell back slightly. Automatically, his right foot shot out to hit the brakes.

Silas slid a laughing glance his way.

Chuckling, Aiden shrugged. "What can I say? I'm used to my car."

Flicking the reins with an easy, practiced movement of his wrists, Silas set the horse off at a trot. Aiden couldn't remember a time he'd felt so exposed. At least in a car, he had the frame around him. Here, he was literally sitting out in the open. There was a window between them and the horse, no doubt to keep the dust and rocks from hitting them, but other than that, they were pretty much visible to anyone who cared to look.

"I want to thank you again for your hospitality, Silas. It really means a lot."

"*Ja*. You're welcome. Gott brought you to us to assist. We are paying back an old debt."

"An old debt? What do you mean?"

Silas sent the mare trotting down another dirt road. "Before Melvin was a member of our church, while he was deciding whether to be Amish or join the *Englisch* world, he became friends with some *Englisch* boys."

Rumspringa. He'd heard of it. Aiden held back from asking questions. Silas was revealing some deeply personal information. He suspected this was not something Silas would have shared were it not for the idea of a debt he owed Aiden.

"One of the young boys my son befriended was being abused by his grandfather. When my son tried to help, the grandfather locked them both in a shed and started to set it on fire."

Aiden remembered that case. "My partner and I were the officers on call. We got the boys out."

"*Ja*. You did more than that. My son had stopped breathing. You did CPR on him. Broke two of his ribs, but he lived. He saw you once, when you came to the hospital to check on him. Eleanor and I were still on our way. We had to find a driver and someone to care for our other children. We never met you before that day, although we did see a picture of you and your partner in the newspaper at the hospital. My son wasn't sure if you were the one who had saved him when we came upon you the other day, but we knew your name."

"I didn't realize he lived that far away."

"*Ja*. He had traveled into the city in a car driven by one of his friends. He has talked of wanting to thank you and your partner for several years."

Aiden felt his throat closing as thoughts of Tim crowded in. He would have been so touched by the story.

"We were glad we could be there." He cleared his throat. "Tim, my partner... He was killed in the line of duty. I know meeting your family, meeting Melvin, and knowing how well he was doing... Well, it would have meant a lot to him."

Aiden understood now why the family was so set on helping them.

"Is that why you trusted us so quickly?"

Silas nodded. "*Ja*. A man who'd save my son without thinking of himself would not kill a young boy. Nor kidnap a woman and her sister."

It wasn't always that simple, but he was glad Silas had decided to help.

Climbing down from the buggy, he thought it had never felt so good to step out of any vehicle. He did appreciate the hospitality, though.

As Silas introduced him around to a few of the other men, he noticed a few speculative glances. The men seemed to accept Silas's explanation that Aiden was visiting them. As far as he could tell, none of the men seemed to recognize him.

The work at the mill was refreshing. Aiden enjoyed working with his hands. The physical labor felt good.

He was beginning to relax when Melvin rushed into the mill. He went to his father immediately and murmured to him. When Silas shot a look his way, Aiden's instincts kicked in and his hand moved to his side to check his service weapon. Which wasn't there.

He strode over to the King men.

Melvin ducked his head in greeting. Now that he knew the story, he could see the resemblance to the youth he'd rescued. He could also see the young man was reticent in nature, which would explain why he hadn't said anything himself about meeting Aiden and Tim previously.

"I was in town," Melvin whispered, his eyes darting around. "I happened to stop by Norma's store, and she talked with me."

Aiden didn't know what the big deal was, but he guessed by the way Silas's mouth dropped open, this wasn't a common occurrence.

"She doesn't often come out of her office," he explained.

"*Ja*. She came out today. And walked right up to me and asked if I'd heard that the doctor had seen the cop accused of murder and kidnapping."

For a few seconds, Aiden's brain froze.

Then the adrenaline kicked in.

"We need to leave. Now."

Sophie had never made jam before. It had not occurred to her what a complex process it really was, and that should have kept her mind occupied.

Instead, she kept walking to the window, watching for Aiden's return.

"Sophie, it's time."

Sighing, she walked back and took her place at the

counter. When Eleanor poured the berries into the large pot, Sophie picked up the old-fashioned potato masher and set to mashing the berries.

Her mouth watered. Strawberries were among her favorite fruits. She liked the raspberries, as well.

Once the berries were all mashed, Eleanor moved the pot to the stove. "We'll add the pectin," she said. She emptied a packet into the mixture and began to stir. "Then we'll let it boil."

Soon the concoction was boiling. Eleanor dumped in sugar. Sophie stirred. Soon it was boiling again.

After a minute, Eleanor announced it was time to finish. She skimmed the top off the mixture and removed it from the heat. Sophie helped her to scoop the jam into jars and put on the lids.

"How long will it take to set?"

"However long it needs. We'll hear the lids pop when the jars are set."

Sophie nodded, idly casting another glance to the window.

The buggy pulled in a lot faster than it had left. Aiden was jumping down before the vehicle had completely halted. He ran for the house, Silas right behind him. When the door banged opened, Eleanor shrieked and swung around, shocked, but she held her tongue. No wonder. There were storm clouds brewing on both men's faces.

Something was wrong.

Stomach clenching, Sophie strove for calm as she approached Aiden. He saw her and grabbed her to him in a quick embrace.

"You're safe," he said, touching her face, her head, to reassure himself. His alarm communicated itself to her.

"What's wrong?"

"In a minute. Where's Celine?"

Celine! The wooden spoon in her hand clattered to the floor. Rushing for the door, she ran outside in her bare feet, hardly even noticing the pain as she raced across the gravel drive to reach the barn. Her sister was helping Mary.

"Celine! You need to come now," she signed.

A mulish expression crossed the girl's face. "I'll come in a minute. We're almost done here."

Sophie cast a glance at Mary and the shearing tool in her hand, then to the almost shorn sheep. Any other time, seeing the sheep with its woolly head and nearly naked body would have made her smile. Now she was on a mission and had no time for her sister's mood.

"No, not later. Now. Aiden's back. Something has happened."

Celine paled and her lips trembled. She left the sheep immediately. Sophie regretted being harsh, but this was urgent.

By the time they returned to the house, Melvin had arrived.

"Okay, please tell us what's happening." Sophie made sure to speak and sign at the same time so all would understand her. She'd interpret whatever they said for Celine.

Eleanor's brow furrowed. "Should the *kind* be here?"

"Yes," Aiden responded. "This effects Celine, so

she needs to be here. I know she's twelve, but this is too important."

Plus, Sophie thought, if Celine was here, they would know where she was.

"I'm here, too." Levi walked down the stairs. His shoulder remained bandaged, but he had some color.

"Should you be up?" Sophie asked him.

"*Ja*, I'm fine. Don't worry about me. Melvin here said that the doctor had a run-in with someone in town who was reading the paper and saw our pictures. I don't know exactly what happened. Somehow, he let it slip that he had seen us."

"Did you ask him?" she gasped. "What about patient confidentiality?"

A look passed between Silas and Aiden.

"We went by his office," Aiden said. "It was still closed up. No one has seen the doctor since yesterday."

Dread seeped through every pore. They had the doctor. Whether it was the police or Phillip's men, she didn't know.

Focus, Sophie.

"What do we do now?"

Aiden shoved his hands in his pockets. His eyes, when they met hers, were steady. "We can't stay here. Silas knows someone else who might let us hide out at his house for a few days. Melvin will help us get there. In the meantime, Silas will report the doctor missing. The local police will search for him."

Sophie heard what he wasn't saying. He believed the doctor had been killed. Sadness weighed on her. Another person affected by their plight. He hadn't said it, but knowing Aiden as she did, the fact that he wasn't going to check on the doctor himself was probably eating at him. He did take the role of protector seriously.

Sometimes too seriously.

"You won't go to Berlin," Levi stated.

"No. Nor do I think you should go with us. Not with your injury."

Celine gasped. Sophie reached out and patted her shoulder. The girl had developed a bit of a crush on Levi.

"Sorry, man. We need to move fast, and I'd hate for your wound to become worse. And I think going to your family's place, well, I don't think that would be wise. They're looking for you, too. If any of us show up at your family's house, it could put them in danger. I wouldn't be surprised if Phillip has someone watching your family. I called my chief on the way here and asked her to check on them. Although, anyone who knows you, knows that you haven't had contact with them for the past few years. It's better if we switch up the plan."

Levi nodded. "I might check into the hospital."

"Really?" They all gaped at him.

"Yeah. If I go there, I'll be protected, cared for, and the rumors of my being kidnapped could be dealt with. Plus, once the news reports that I have been rescued without you, it will be obvious that we didn't go to my family. Even if the police come, I can honestly tell them I have no knowledge of where you are and that you did not kidnap me, nor did you shoot me or hurt the girls."

"What if they arrest you?" Celine asked once Sophie finished interpreting.

He shrugged. "I'll live. And Aiden can always clear me once this situation is done."

That was putting a lot of faith in their success.

No. This was faith that God would bring the whole mess to a close.

Lord, Your will be done. Please protect all who we have come into contact with.

The next half hour was spent scrambling, gathering up what they might need for their journey. They were still headed in the direction of Berlin, but Silas was sending them to a man who lived on the outskirts of town. He was an older man who lived alone, his own family having all been killed in an accident fifteen years earlier. He'd never remarried. Silas seemed to feel he would welcome the company.

"We don't want to leave you without a buggy," Aiden said to Silas and Eleanor.

"*Nee*, don't worry. We must help each other, ain't so?" Silas replied. "We have a second buggy if we need it. It is no bother for us to loan it to you."

Eleanor handed them a basket with food. "Including some jam. It's not set yet, but it will be in a couple of hours."

They thanked them before climbing into the buggy. Aiden squeezed inside with Sophie and Celine while Melvin clambered up on the bench to drive.

"I don't want anyone to see me from the road," he murmured. "Nor do I want to show the world that I'm armed." He opened his jacket.

Sure enough, his service weapon was back in the

holster. It struck her as odd to see a gun on a man dressed Plain.

They pulled onto the drive and then the dirt road. Dust rose up and tickled her nose. She sneezed. Aiden offered her a facial tissue from the backpack he'd brought along. They must have come from Eleanor. She didn't recall having them when they had started out on the journey.

"Should we call your chief?" She kept her voice low, even though Celine couldn't hear her. She wasn't sure how much sound would travel from the buggy to Melvin.

He shook his head. "In fact, I threw that phone out. I'd already used it several times. We still have one more. I left the third with Levi."

"Will you call her?"

He didn't answer at first. She waited. He would tell her once the answer was formulated in his mind. She'd learned that he wasn't one who liked to answer off the cuff.

Finally, he spoke. "I'm not comfortable with calling her yet. She says she knows who the mole is, but I'm positive they've got the wrong person. I can't promise that, but my gut says I'm right. So I'm waiting. I did put her number into this phone, just in case you need to contact her."

She didn't like the implication. If she needed to call the chief, then he would be unable to make the call himself. The idea of him being hurt or killed struck her in the pit of her stomach. She loved—

No, no and no. She did not love him. He was helping

them. She was grateful for him. That was the extent of her feelings for him.

Liar.

She was not ready to examine her feelings or the consequences of them any further, not while they were literally running for their lives.

But she had a feeling that once they were safe, if they were ever safe again, it would be too late.

Because Aiden would leave, and she would be alone with her heart in pieces.

Stop. She couldn't bear these thoughts.

She opened her mouth to say something, words that were never uttered.

The rear window shattered.

THIRTEEN

"**G**et down!" Aiden shoved Celine to the floor of the buggy. Sobbing wildly, she shrank down, her arms circling her knees.

Sophie slid off the seat and wrapped herself protectively around her sister.

"Melvin! Are you hurt?" The buggy had picked up speed but didn't seem to be out of control, so he was fairly confident that the man was uninjured.

"Nee!" Melvin shouted back.

"Stay here." Praying that he would be able to manage it, Aiden reached through the front opening and grabbed the bench. He pulled himself through the opening and swung his legs over so that he was sitting beside Melvin, who shifted over so they could both fit.

Aiden removed his service weapon from the holster. He saw his companion's eyes widen in alarm. "I'm sorry, Melvin. I know your family wouldn't use a gun, but I will protect the women and you if I can."

Melvin gulped and didn't say anything.

A second shot rang out, dinging the back of the buggy.

"Sophie!"

"We're not hurt. He missed us!"

Momentarily, he sagged against the seat. They were fine. They weren't hurt. And they would stay that way.

Straightening, he leaned and twisted his torso to see if he could catch a glimpse of the car roaring up behind them. There was no way they'd be able to outrun them.

Aiden aimed and fired. The front passenger-side tire blew out.

He could see the driver of the car struggling to regain control of the vehicle as it swerved back and forth. It nicked the guardrail with the front fender, but it kept moving. Slower now that the wheel was riding on a flat tire. But still coming.

"We have trouble!" Melvin shouted.

More? The last thing they needed was more trouble.

They were quickly approaching train tracks. The light began to blink. They were going to be stopped by a train. They'd die for sure.

Not. Going. To. Happen.

"Go around the crossing gates!"

Melvin did a double take. "What?"

"We have time," he shouted. "The train isn't here yet. If we stop, we'll all die. Go around the gates."

Melvin's face tightened. His hands gripped the reins and he steered the horse around the gates. The buggy rocked precariously at the speed they were traveling.

A third shot glanced off the bottom of the buggy. The vehicle swayed. Then with a creak and a groan, the back right wheel fell off. They'd shot the axle. The buggy had landed with the back end still on the tracks. No amount of pulling would move it.

"Get out!"

He and Melvin both jumped down and he bolted to the side to assist first Celine and then Sophie out while Melvin freed the horse. The train whistle blew. It was close. Too close. Melvin smacked the hind end of the mare with a yell. She took off and ran a few feet away. Enough that she'd be safe. Sophie and Celine grabbed hands and ran as fast as they could.

Once everyone was clear, Aiden sprinted off the tracks.

The car skidded to a halt on the other side.

Reaching the others, he pushed them a little farther away. The thundering of the train was upon them. He looked back in time to see the freight train plow into the buggy. He winced. The buggy was no match for the locomotive. It splintered and shattered. Shards of it rained down over them.

The group stood, shocked, for a few seconds. Somehow, through all that, he and Melvin had both kept their hats. He shook his head at the irrelevant thought.

Then the reality of their situation sank in.

"We gotta move. The train is blocking us from their view, but once it's gone, that car is going to come after us."

Celine looked like she was going to cry, but to his surprise she held it together. So did Sophie.

"We'll have to jog at first," Melvin stated. "Can you keep up?"

"What about the horse?" Celine asked.

Melvin smiled at the girl. "Don't worry about the mare. She'll go home on her own."

She bit her lip. "Couldn't someone ride her?"

"*Nee*. Amish don't use their horses for riding. She's never had anyone on her. She'd be likely to throw you off."

"Oh." Her disappointment was so palpable and precious, and the adults all hid smiles.

"You can run, Celine. We'll stop and walk if it gets too much." He waited until she nodded in reluctant agreement before motioning for Melvin to lead the way. Aiden let the others go ahead of him so he could keep aware of any dangers coming up behind them. Anything that tried to get to them would have to go through him first.

He reached down and made sure that his gun was still in his holster.

It was. What was missing was his wallet. Somehow he'd lost it. Had it fallen out? Or had he not put it in his pocket that morning? Wherever it was, it was too late to go back for it. He didn't know what he'd do if he had to prove his identity. Everything that identified him as Aiden Forster, a cop from Talon Hill, was in that piece of leather.

He'd have to worry about that later.

They kept to the dirt roads and the wooded areas. After about thirty minutes of jogging, Celine cried out that she needed to slow down.

"Let's walk for a little while. Let everyone get their breath back," Aiden called out. No one argued. Celine gave him a look of profound gratitude.

"You're her new hero," Sophie remarked.

He shrugged, uncomfortable with the statement. "I'm not a hero. Just a cop, doing my job."

"If you say so." She let it drop. "This whole mess we're in, is it the worst one you've ever been in?"

He shook his head. "Not even close. My days as a soldier were way worse. We were always in danger. And there were nights where we would sleep while land mines were blowing up within hearing distance. It was nasty stuff."

Her arm brushed his. "I don't think I could bear it if something happened to Celine."

Where had that come from?

"I lost my whole family, except for her. She's so much younger than I am that we've never really been close. And some of that was definitely on me. I put so much emphasis and focus on moving up in my career. I don't think it was worth it."

"It's one of those things that we have to learn, even though it's painful." Like he had to learn to live without his sister. "I lost my sister, but I'm grateful that I know she's still alive."

Sophie enjoyed jogging, but not like this.

After walking for half an hour, they were back to running. Then they walked. Then jogged. She might never willingly jog in the afternoon again. She felt bad for Celine. She could tell her sister was feeling the strain of the exercise. Her face was beet red and she was breathing in huge gulps. She raised her eyebrows at Aiden and jerked her head at Celine. He understood and called a halt.

"I think this is a good place to rest for a bit," he announced.

"Finally!" Celine flopped down against a tree without looking to see what she was landing on.

Sophie bit back a smile.

"I know this area," Melvin said. "There's a store not far from here. What say I go into town and get us some food?"

"What if someone sees you?" Celine asked, her face filled with fear.

Melvin laughed. "People know me. They know where I live. If someone wanted to find me, they'd walk to Mamm and Dat's *haus*, and there I'd be."

"I hate that we're dragging you into this," Sophie exclaimed.

"*Nee*. It is *gut*. I had a debt to pay, and I'm paying it."

Sophie had no idea what he was talking about.

"There wasn't a debt, you know." Aiden settled down next to her on the grass. He looked at Melvin. They were seated in a wooded area. The sun coming through the trees cast shadows over their faces. It was difficult to read the expression in his gaze. His voice, though, was warm and gentle. "Your dad talked to me. I remember you. I did what I had to do."

"*Ja*. I know. You saved my life. You saved the life of my friend."

"I didn't realize you two had met before," she commented.

Aiden flashed her a grin. "I didn't know we had,

either. Until his dad reminded me of a couple of teens Tim and I had pulled from a fire a few years back."

"*Nee*, there's more than that," Melvin insisted. He turned to Sophie, his shyness forgotten in his desire to set things straight. "My friend, his *grossdawdi* was a bad person. He would beat him and threaten horrible things. He locked us inside a shed and set it on fire. Aiden rescued us and gave me CPR." He looked straight at Aiden. "I'd stopped breathing."

Aiden flushed, but nodded. "Yeah. Your dad reminded me that I had broken a couple of your ribs."

Melvin waved it away. "*Ach*. That didn't matter. I would have died. You saved me. I will never forget it."

So he was someone else's hero, too.

Sophie's stomach chose that moment to emit a long, drawn-out growl.

Melvin rose. "I will go and get some food, *ja*?"

He left. Sophie looked over at Celine. She'd fallen asleep sitting up against the tree.

"She's been a trouper," Aiden said.

"I know. She's been through things no twelve-year-old child should deal with."

Aiden's hand covered hers where it was on the ground. "Hey, Sophie, don't worry about her. She is a strong, resilient kid. She'll pull through. You'll see."

In the dim light, she could just make out his face. Suddenly, sitting so close, she remembered sitting with him on the steps of the King house. And she remembered the kiss that almost was.

She wanted that kiss.

They were in the middle of the woods, still running

for their lives, and all she could think about was how close his lips were to hers. It would be so easy to lean over and touch his lips. So easy.

Of course, she'd never do such a thing. No, that would be too bold for her. Instead, she'd sit here feeling the warmth of his presence and longing—

Her thoughts stopped as Aiden bent closer and kissed her.

A gentle kiss. Then he kissed her again. The warmth that spread through her had nothing to do with the weather and everything to do with this man.

He backed away. Her eyes fluttered open.

He was chastising himself for giving in to the kiss. She could tell.

"Don't think about it, Aiden. We've both wanted it." She couldn't believe she was so bold.

"You're right. But that doesn't mean it should have happened. I'm protecting you. I think you might feel confused."

Okay, now she was mad. Standing up, she moved away from him.

"Sophie?"

"Who are you to tell me how I feel, Aiden Forster?" She stomped a few feet away, then stomped back. "I'm a grown woman. I don't go around kissing people. It's not my way. For you to suggest that I was swayed by the situation is, frankly, insulting."

He laughed and got to his feet. "Now we know you have a temper. Look, I didn't mean anything by it. It's not the right time."

"So?"

Was he suggesting that there might be a chance for them? A second later, he dashed that hope. "But even if we weren't in danger, Sophie, I'm not the man for you. For anyone. I have too much baggage, and my job makes my life crazy. I have no business being involved with anyone."

She swallowed. That was fairly clear. She needed to do a better job of guarding her heart. They sat again, but they faced each other with space between them, removing the temptation.

She was relieved when Melvin returned. He had purchased sandwiches and water. They ate in silence. The only noise was chewing and swallowing.

When they had completed their meal, it was a weary group that resumed walking.

"It's just up ahead," Melvin called finally.

The house itself didn't look promising. In fact, it almost looked like it was vacant.

She hesitated as the others started toward the steps. When Aiden quirked his eyebrow at her, she lifted her chin and strode up to the door. Silas had vouched for the man who lived here. What could go wrong?

FOURTEEN

The front door swung open as they approached. A man in his fifties stood watching them approach. His face was solemn, his chin covered with a full salt-and-pepper beard.

"'Lo, Melvin. What's going on?"

"Ivan. Dat wanted me to bring over some guests. Seems to be we need some help. Could we come in?"

Ivan looked them over slowly before he nodded.

"Ja. Cumme."

They filed into his house. Despite its outward appearance, the interior of the home was charming. It was clean, and though the furniture was sparse, it was a comfortable spot.

For what felt like the hundredth time, they explained the parts of their story that could be revealed. Ivan asked very pointed questions. So pointed, in fact, that Sophie was positive he was going to say, no, they couldn't stay.

In that event, she had no idea what they would do. They had run through their options. They were out of friends in the area, and neither she nor Aiden had family they could turn to. Plus, he still couldn't return to the precinct.

"*Ja*, you can stay." He shrugged. She was so tired and overly emotional she thought she might cry. "Melvin, you staying the night, too?"

"*Ja*. I will stay tonight, but tomorrow I need to return home first thing."

An hour later, she was in bed, safe and warm. Her lids were heavy. Then she heard a heavy thumping sound outside her window. It was footsteps. She walked to the window and knelt down so she wouldn't be seen. Peering down, she saw a familiar dark head.

Aiden was out there, alone, pacing on the porch. She was tempted to join him but decided against it. The last time they were alone together, they'd kissed. She remembered the sting of his response. He didn't want her to kiss him. He didn't want a relationship, period.

That was fine with her.

She was too tired, anyway. She needed sleep. Stumbling back to her bed, she lay awake for an hour before finally falling to sleep.

The next morning dawned sunny and warm. Melvin left immediately after breakfast. Ivan had given him a ride home in his buggy. By the time the older man returned, the sun was already cooking the earth below. It would be a scorcher by noon. By nine o'clock, it was hot enough that Sophie commented that her skin was melting. Aiden laughed.

He was amazed that she was so unconscious of how lovely she was. Even dressed Amish, with her glorious hair hidden, her beauty shone through. It made him wish he was a man who was fit to take a bride.

No longer did he delude himself into believing he had no feelings for her. His comments the night before regarding her feelings not being real had more to do with protecting himself than to do with her.

He'd been protecting himself for so long he wasn't sure how to go about changing it. Janet, although she certainly hadn't meant to help him, had shown him that his life was not one a woman who was worthy would accept. Janet might not have been worthy, but Sophie was. She was more than worthy.

And then there was Celine. Celine was a precious little girl who would grow up into a beautiful woman. Any man who married Sophie would take on the role of surrogate father to her. He wished it could be him.

Frustrated, he shoved the idea away. He wouldn't waste his time with these absurd dreams anymore. He had duties.

As was his habit, he walked the perimeter of the property several times that day. He hadn't seen anything yet, but that didn't mean anything. These guys were sneaky.

"Hey, stranger."

Sophie walked toward him with her long-legged stride. She covered the ground quickly and with a confidence he found alluring.

"Hey, yourself. What do you have there?" He indicated her hand.

"I'm a firm believer in making lists." She held out the pen and paper in her grip.

"I was thinking about my uncle and this situation we're in. So I thought, since we're stranded here, maybe we could go over the possible moles at your precinct and make a list. I know you said the person they've pinpointed couldn't be it. Maybe we can find someone who makes more sense."

It wasn't a half-bad idea. And like she said, they didn't have anything pressing to do at the moment. Wandering inside, they sat at the table and he ran through a list of the personnel at his precinct.

When Sophie wrote the chief's name on the list, he laughed.

"You've got to be kidding me."

"Mostly I am. But I will note that every time you've called her, someone has found us. It could be said that it was awfully coincidental. Plus, the fact that the mole still hasn't been correctly identified."

"You have some good points, but the chief would actually want me to come back if she was. She could have me meet with an accident. And she's the one who told me to stay away and not call often. No, I have to believe it's someone else."

She shrugged. "I'm just trying to help."

"And I appreciate it. Really. Let's go on to the next name."

Name by name, they eliminated each person. Finally, there were only three names left.

"I need a break," he said, standing. He stretched his arms over his head. "I'm going to walk around again."

"I'll come with you. Celine is taking a nap, so I have nothing else to do."

"Nothing better, you mean."

"That, too." He'd miss bantering with her when this was done.

They walked around the yard, talking and laughing.

When they returned to the house, they were startled to see a police cruiser in the yard. Ivan was there, arguing with the men. Celine was crying.

The two cops fastened their gazes on Aiden.

"Adam Steele." One of them drew his gun and pointed it directly at Aiden. "You're under arrest for the murder of Cash Wellman. And the kidnapping—"

"He didn't kidnap me!" Sophie stormed up to them. "And his name is not Adam Steele. It's Aiden Forster."

"Ma'am, you've been taken in by a con man. It's obvious he didn't kidnap you. But as for him," the officer jerked his thumb at Aiden, "Adam, or Aiden, whoever he is, well, we're taking him in."

"Shouldn't we take them both in?" the other cop asked.

"No. She's in the clear. We had someone say they saw her at the time Wellman was killed. They have her vehicle going through a traffic light. She's good."

"He was with me!"

The officers both looked at her with pity. As they started to take him away, Aiden was protesting that he was an undercover cop.

"Fine. Prove it. Where's your identification?"

He didn't have any. He didn't want to implicate the King family. If he sent the cops there to find his identification, it could cause real trouble for them. His best bet was to get in touch with Chief Daniels. She could clear up the matter real quick.

"Look, I lost my wallet. I could call my chief."

"Sure, sure, call your chief at the station. Or you can call your lawyer."

Sophie watched in horror as the cops pushed Aiden into their car and drove him away.

"Sophie, what should we do?"

She turned to face her sister. "Let me think for a minute."

She paced the room. What could they do? Ivan didn't have a phone.

Wait a minute. He might not have a phone, but she did. Running upstairs, she grabbed the phone that Aiden had programmed with the chief's number. With trembling fingers, she opened the phone, then found the chief's contact information. While she waited for the phone to ring, she said a prayer under her breath.

The phone rang once, twice. The phone was answered midring.

"Daniels."

"Chief Daniels. You don't know me, but my name is Sophie Larson."

"Larson. You're Phillip's niece." The voice sharpened. "Why isn't Aiden calling me? Has something happened to him?"

"Yes, ma'am." Briefly she described the cops picking him up and him not having his wallet to prove his identity. "Ma'am, I don't know how they knew we were here. I don't think we've seen anyone."

"Well, clearly someone did see you. Don't worry, Miss Larson. I'm going to go and get him out of jail.

You sit tight. I'll call this number back when I have news to share."

Relief poured through her. The chief believed her. She had been dreading talking with her, fearing that she would believe this was a trick or a prank of some kind.

When the chief disconnected, Sophie went downstairs. She couldn't sit still. Every few minutes, she glanced at the phone to see if the chief had tried to call back. How long would this take? Would the chief be able to call the other station, or would she actually have to drive there to release Aiden?

Without his presence, she felt vulnerable.

She missed him. He'd only been gone an hour, but she felt the hole his absence made.

Celine seemed to be missing him, as well. The preteen had been sulking. Whenever Sophie saw her pouting face, she wanted to roll her eyes. No one did sulking like Celine.

Sophie was completely unprepared for Celine to spring up out of her seat. "This is stupid. I can't believe we're just standing here doing nothing."

"Not nothing. I've called his chief."

Celine scoffed. "Yeah, that seems to be working. I'm done." Celine yanked the prayer *kapp* off her head and tossed it down.

She stormed out of the house. Sophie apologized to Ivan before running after her sister.

She was nowhere to be found. Where could she have gone. She clenched her teeth. Celine knew better than to run off. Sophie called her name before remembering Celine couldn't hear anything.

"I can't believe this girl." She looked around the yard. Nothing. Twenty minutes later, she was still searching. Her anger had given way to worry. Anxiety built up inside her. Her sister was nowhere to be seen. Ivan and she split up to increase the likelihood of finding her.

A bad feeling crept over Sophie. Suddenly she was sure that they wouldn't find her here. Had she left the property in her irritation?

Sophie set off down the road, eyes scanning the area for any sign of her sister. Her sister had been wearing a light blue dress with a white apron. Her bright red hair would be easy to spot without the *kapp* on it.

As she was moving down the street, a car purred up beside her.

She glanced over. And froze.

Phillip Larson smiled at her from the passenger seat. Despite the smile, his eyes were stone cold. A shark, she thought again. A gun was held steady in his very capable hand. It was pointed directly at her. She had no doubt that if he decided to fire, he would hit his target.

"Dear niece, I am so glad to see you. I'm hoping you'll join me. Hmm?"

If she got in that car, she was dead. What were her chances of running? Not much, but at least it would be a small chance. If she was shot, maybe she could get far enough away that someone might find her and take her to the hospital.

"I hope you are not thinking of leaving, Sophie. I would hate for you to choose badly. And so would Celine."

Celine. Her blood ran cold. "What have you done with her?"

"Nothing. Yet. It's all your choice what happens."

"She's alive? I want to see her."

"She's alive. She looks charming in her Amish dress. I wonder why she didn't have her bonnet on?"

He knew. He knew that Celine wasn't wearing the *kapp*. He did have her. Was she too late?

When Phillip waved his gun at her, she knew she had no choice. She had to go with him. She entered the car. When he closed the door, she felt like a wild animal tossed into a cage.

They drove for a long time, so long she lost track of the twists and turns as they continued on. A second vehicle joined them. That must be where Celine was being held.

At some point, she drifted into an exhausted doze. She jerked awake. They were at a house that she had never seen before. It was as large as Phillip's house in Talon Hill, but much more secluded.

Phillip pulled her out of the car and dragged her up a set of stairs. "I'm very annoyed with you, my dear. You've put me through a great deal of stress. I was just going to kill you. That's what I'd normally do, but now I'm wondering if I can't find a more lucrative use for you."

Sophie began to shiver uncontrollably. She was in over her head, with no way out.

FIFTEEN

"I'm a cop," Aiden insisted as the officers pulled him from their car and into the station.

"Yeah? If you are, that means you're a bad cop."

How could he get out of this? "No! Not a bad cop. I was undercover. Look, you can call my chief. She'll explain everything. But if I don't get out of here, the woman that I was with, and likely her sister, will both die."

"Aww, you're bringing tears to my eyes," the officer sneered. The other one smirked.

When he was released, he was definitely talking to their superior. No matter what he said, the officers jeered at him, refusing to give credence to his words.

Despite the fact that two women might die. Oh, yeah. He wasn't going to overlook this. Not when so much was at stake.

They put him into a holding cell. He paced and fumed, his mind fraught with various scenarios in which Sophie was found or hurt. All because he wasn't there.

He wasn't with her, but God still was. With his whole

heart, he cried out to God, begging Him to step in and protect Sophie and Celine. *Please Lord. I love her. I love them both. I know that I can't keep them, but I know they are precious to You. Please, save them. And if it's all right, help me get out of here so I can go to them. Even if it's only to make sure they are well and to say goodbye.*

He had no idea how long he prayed. It could have been thirty minutes, it could have been an hour. When the door opened, he looked up, blinking. His vision was blurry. Realizing his eyes were damp, he hastily wiped his sleeve across his face.

A familiar figure walked through the door. His visitor was an attractive African American woman. Her skin was smooth and seemed ageless. Her dark brown eyes were sharp. Chief Wanda Daniels wore her authority well. She commanded respect and got it.

"Chief!" Aiden strode to the door.

Behind her he could see the two officers who'd brought him in. Both looked like they'd been force-fed vinegar. Neither would meet his gaze.

"Lieutenant," Chief Daniels greeted him. "Sophie Larson called me. I'm getting you out of here."

"Chief, is Sophie safe?"

"I have no idea where she is. When I tried to call her back, there was no answer. We will go find her. I'm a bit worried myself. After she called, I discovered proof that my personal assistant had intercepted the call and relayed the conversation to someone in Pennsylvania."

"Larson," he ground out, his muscles tightening.

"I'm afraid so. You were correct. We had the wrong person. Let's go find Miss Larson and her sister."

Chief Daniels had officers sent to Ivan's place to search for Celine and Sophie. Aiden's heart nearly stopped when they were nowhere to be found.

The chief also had officers sent to Phillip Larson's residence. There was no one there. It appeared that Larson had taken off in a hurry, judging by the half-eaten plate of spaghetti left on his kitchen table. The man was fastidious about keeping things neat and tidy.

Something mighty important must have called him away.

Something like the woman he'd been searching for having been located.

Aiden's gut tightened. He shoved away images of Sophie and Celine being at Larson's mercy. They wouldn't help him recover the woman he had fallen in love with. It was so easy to admit now. And he was so close to losing her.

No, he wasn't going there.

Brandi, the woman in custody, refused to speak at first. Aiden informed her that she was going to be held responsible for anything that happened to Sophie and Celine. She'd been the chief's personal assistant long enough to know he meant what he said.

"As well as the death of Cash Wellman," the chief added.

Aiden crossed his arms over his chest and scowled at Brandi. "I'm thinking you look good for the death penalty."

Brandi began weeping. "I didn't mean for anyone to get hurt. It's not my fault."

"Whose fault is it, if you don't mind telling me?"

She sniffed and wiped her nose on the tissue Daniels handed her. "My boyfriend, Sam Kinney, works for Phillip Larson. When Larson realized where I worked, I was told to spy or else my boyfriend would be in for it. Honest. I would have never done it if I didn't have to."

Sam Kinney. He knew that name. He made his living running cons and selling drugs. He couldn't believe someone in Brandi's position would fall for a man like that.

"My partner, Tim," Aiden started. Brandi froze, giving him a deer-in-the-headlights expression. He knew she was involved. "That ambush was on your information, wasn't it?"

She finally admitted it was. "Yes."

This woman was the one who gave Phillip the information about where his partner would be that night. She must have intercepted his call for backup. She was the one responsible for his death. A sudden thought occurred to him.

"Lawson knew that I was undercover, didn't he?"

"He knew. He was watching you. Having you kill the Larson sisters was a test, but he was already planning on you bailing to save them."

Phillip had been playing with them the whole time, using this selfish woman to undercut their every move.

The interview would have to be continued later. They were running out of time.

Brandi made one more confession. "He has them now."

His blood ran cold. "Excuse me?"

"Phillip Larson. After the police picked you up, he

used the information I gave him. My boyfriend told me he's found his nieces."

"Where are they?"

"My boyfriend says they're on their way to Phillip's second house."

It took a few minutes to get the information from her, but once they had it, they wasted no time. Chief Daniels gathered several teams of officers. Aiden joined her in her car. It was almost dark by the time they arrived. Phillip's house was off the road a way.

"We have to assume there are alarms."

Judson, an officer who possessed a vast knowledge of alarms and how to dismantle them, proved very useful. There was indeed an alarm. He disabled it without tripping it. On foot, the teams moved in on the house.

They gained entry through an unlocked cellar door. The team moved into the house and spread out. The first three doors they tried were empty. On the fourth, Aiden opened the door and found it was occupied. The familiar red head shot up.

Celine was tied to a chair. Her face was bruised, but otherwise she appeared uninjured.

"Aiden!"

He held a finger to his lips to silence her. She nodded to show she understood. When she was released, she flew to him and threw her arms around him. He hugged her back quickly, then set her back. Bending so they were on eye level and she could better read his lips, he spoke to her rapidly, hoping she'd understand.

"I need you to go with this officer," he said as a

young policewoman stepped forward. "She's going to get you to a safe place while I go and find Sophie."

She clutched at his arm. "Don't let him hurt her!"

"I'll do my best for her." He couldn't promise any more than that.

He just prayed he wasn't too late.

The officer led Celine away. When Aiden was sure that she had made it out, he refocused all his energy on saving Sophie.

Slowly he moved into the hallway, his weapon out and ready. The officer ahead of him was in charge of peering around corners and making sure the area was clear. After each room was cleared, they moved on.

"Wait," Aiden whispered. The other two men halted. He pointed his finger up. They listened. Upstairs they could hear voices.

A male voice. Angry. Demanding.

A female voice. Quieter, but the defiance was there.

Sophie. She was alive. Hearing her voice, he nearly wilted against the wall behind him. He maintained his composure, and his patience, with effort. Every instinct urged him to race up the stairs, burst into the room where she and Phillip were, and rescue her.

His experience told him if he wanted to keep her alive, he needed to use his head and not his heart. It was difficult, but he waited.

Finally, just when he thought he couldn't take it anymore, they moved. An officer outside of the house had confirmed that Sophie and Phillip were alone in the room. The sniper had his weapon ready, but hadn't been able to get off a shot without endangering Sophie.

It was up to them. They were at the door. Judson threw the door open and Aiden charged in.

"Police! Drop your gun and step away, Larson!" Aiden shouted, holding his weapon up, ready to shoot as he advanced into the room. The others filed in behind him, but he kept his glare trained on his prey. He refused to look at Sophie, fearful that she would distract him.

Phillip sneered. "You wouldn't dare shoot me. You're too soft. You might hit Sophie."

Aiden was a trained sniper, but still sweat trickled down his neck. Shooting a gun was never something to take lightly. Every shot had consequences.

"Give it up, Larson. You're surrounded."

Phillip paused, but only for a second. "It doesn't matter. You'll let me go because at a single command from me, the younger sister will die. And if you don't back off, this one will die, too."

With a yank, he pulled Sophie in front of him, blocking Aiden's shot.

Furious, Aiden allowed his weapon to drop slightly, knowing he couldn't shoot now. He moved to the right. Larson moved with him, forcing Sophie to turn, as well. Aiden took another two steps. So did Larson. Phillip Larson's back was now to the door.

Sophie whimpered. Not for herself, he was sure. "Sophie, don't believe him. We have Celine. She's safe."

At his words, Phillip's grip on Sophie tightened. He pressed the gun tightly against her temple. "It matters not. I still have this one. Let me go, or I will shoot. You know me well enough to know that's no empty threat."

He did.

His heart was heavy in his chest. What other choice did he have? Anger burned. He had failed her.

Stop it! He lowered his gun, keeping Sophie and Phillip in his sight. Any chance, no matter how small, he would take. Any chance that wouldn't risk Sophie getting hurt. He had no other alternative.

Knowing the situation was out of his control, he began to silently pray. His prayers were jumbled, probably incoherent, but God would understand.

Daniels stepped quietly into the room behind Phillip. Her feet were almost completely silent. Almost… Phillip whirled his gun around. Now that the gun was no longer pressed against her temple, Sophie reacted, biting down on the arm across her chest. With a yell, Phillip released her. Aiden snatched her from Phillip before he could reclaim her and jerked her behind him.

Phillip brought up his gun, roaring in fury, and shot. Aiden caught the shot in his arm. Though he flinched, his arm didn't waver. When Phillip aimed and put his finger on the trigger for a second shot, Aiden fired.

Phillip staggered and dropped to the ground. Aiden didn't need to know that the man who had killed Tim and who had been about to kill the woman he loved was dead.

There was no joy in killing him. No matter how bad the criminal was, Aiden was always keenly aware of the fact that a soul was inside the shell of a body. Ending a life was never something to take lightly.

He bowed his head for a brief moment.

Someone was at his shoulder. A soft hand settled there.

Sophie.

He could breathe again.

There was blood on Aiden's arm.

She wanted to look at it, make sure he was all right. When he whirled to face her, all thoughts faded under the heat of his gaze. When he reached for her, she forgot completely that they weren't alone. Instead, she burrowed into his embrace and released the torrent of tears welled up inside her.

It was over.

Phillip, the uncle she'd never really known, was dead. He had killed so many people, and had tried to kill her and her sister. And because of the man she was hugging, he had failed. Now he would never be able to hurt another person.

She should have been thrilled.

As her tears subsided, though, a new panic set in.

Aiden would leave. She had known it the whole time, and now it would become a reality. Unless she could talk him out of it.

But not here. Not where so many people were watching. If she could get him alone.

First, she had to check on Celine. She backed away from his arms, wishing she could stay there and knowing she couldn't. It was the hardest thing to do, but she forced herself to smile up at him as if her heart wasn't shattering into a million pieces.

"I need to see Celine."

He searched her face, frowning in concern. She didn't think he even realized what he was doing when he smoothed her hair away from her face and tucked a strand behind her ear.

"I'll take you to her."

He stepped back. Suddenly she was faced with a stranger. The Aiden she knew had withdrawn. Heart in her throat, she walked with him, not knowing what to say to break the sudden tension.

She longed for some kind of physical contact. He always made her feel so safe. He didn't even take her hand, though.

She braced herself against the emotional tidal wave brewing inside her. Anger, joy, fear, relief. And a healthy dose of frustration aimed directly at the man beside her. His face was devoid of emotion. It was a mask, she understood, but why couldn't he give them a chance.

Biting her lip to keep her emotions at bay, Sophie walked on. When she saw Celine sitting on the hood of a police cruiser, she released her hold on her emotions and rushed to her side. The sisters cried together. Her heart was suddenly full of gratitude. God had been faithful. He'd brought them all out of it alive.

She leaned back so she could sign. There was just enough light provided by the running lights on the cruiser.

"I love you. I'm so glad God kept us safe."

Celine ducked her head for a moment before signing back.

"I love you, too. I'm sorry. It's my fault he caught us."

She smoothed back her sister's hair. "Silly. He was going to keep coming for us. It didn't matter what we did. He wouldn't stop until he was in jail or dead."

Celine stilled. "Is he dead?"

"Yes. He won't come after us ever again."

They continued signing to each other for a few more minutes. Sophie knew that signing was more comfortable than risking using her voice right now. Without her processors, Celine had no idea how loud she was speaking. Plus, this was a private moment.

"Ma'am." One of the officers approached her. "Chief Daniels asked me to help you get settled in a hotel."

She sighed. It was too late for her to start the trek back to Chicago tonight. Did she even want to return home? She didn't know. And now was not the time to make those decisions. They were both exhausted. Sleep and a good meal, in that order, were what they needed now.

"Thank you, Officer. We'd appreciate the ride. I want to talk with Aiden for a moment. Any idea where I can find him?"

He pointed her in his direction, and she found him talking on his phone. When she heard the name Levi and realized that their friend was also on his way home, she smiled. Her smile left when she met Aiden's eyes. She couldn't read anything in his eyes, on his face. She shivered.

Maybe she should leave him alone and try later.

No. She rejected that idea immediately. He'd just build up his walls and fortify himself against her. If they were going to talk, it needed to be now. Then she'd know if she was going back to Chicago tomorrow and staying there, or if there was anything for her here in Ohio.

Chicago lost much of its charm when compared to losing Aiden.

He hung up and waited for her to speak.

"I see you got your arm taken care of."

"Oh, yeah." He flicked a glance at the bandage there. "It's not much of a battle wound. It won't hold me back."

"Thanks for coming for us."

The smallest smile tilted his lips, bringing a tiny spark of hope to life inside her. "I told you I'd get you through this. Thanks for calling the chief. She was able to get me out of jail. And prove my innocence."

"Good. That's good." She searched for another topic. Why was this so hard? "Did they find the mole?"

His jaw hardened. "Yep. Turns out one of Larson's goons was dating the chief's secretary."

Her jaw dropped. "Seriously?"

"She's the reason that Larson found you after you contacted the chief. She's also responsible for Tim's death."

His partner. The one he blamed himself for.

"So you know you didn't fail him, right? Someone you should have been able to trust was working against you."

He scuffed his foot on the driveway. "Yeah, I know that. Look, Sophie, you're safe now. Your uncle's gone. You can go home. I—"

Oh, no, she wasn't going to let him dismiss her that easy.

"That's it? After all we've been through, you're just going to walk away?"

"What did you expect? Sophie, I am a cop. I was

trying to rescue you and bring a murderer to justice. That's it."

How dare he make a mockery of what happened between them.

"That's it?" she hissed. "You've got to be kidding me. Is this the way you normally work? Holding hands, kissing? That how you deal with women in your protection?"

His expression closed in even more. She took two steps, bringing her toes an inch from his.

"I don't think it is, Aiden. I think you felt something, just like I did. And I think that you are so afraid of failing others that you refuse to give in to your feelings. Is that what it is?"

"You're wrong. There were no feelings. I was only comforting you."

Her heart was breaking inside her chest, and there was nothing she could do. She placed a hand gently on his cheek. He stiffened. She started to withdraw her hand but stopped when his hand covered hers. A war was going on inside him. Sophie could see him fighting. Then their eyes met. And held. When he leaned down to kiss her, she met him halfway.

Her heart fluttered in her chest. The kiss went on for a few seconds before he brought it to an end and moved away from her. She could see the emotion on his face now. He wasn't able to mask his feelings. When he'd kissed her, she thought maybe there was a chance. That hope faded as she looked into his eyes.

When she saw despair, her breath caught in her throat.

"I can't. Sophie, I can't be the man for you. I have too much baggage. I'm not a good bargain for any woman."

She used the last argument she had. "I know you have things to work through. I'm willing to wait. But please don't close the door on us. Aiden, I love you."

At first, she thought she'd gotten through to him.

Then he shook his head. "There is no us. Have a safe trip back to Chicago."

When he walked away, he carried her heart with him.

SIXTEEN

Aiden rapped on the door, his stomach quivering like he'd swallowed several large and very active frogs. He tugged at the tie he was wearing, already regretting putting it on this morning. Sweat was beading on his forehead. He wasn't sure if it was from nerves or the heat. It was sweltering in the dim hallway.

What was he doing here? This journey was bound to end in failure.

Again.

He almost turned around and left. Almost. But he had a promise to keep. And he would never be at peace or be able to return to the woman he loved until this step was taken.

If she'd accept him now.

He grimaced. It had been three weeks since he'd last seen Sophie. Three weeks in which he'd focused all his energies on completing the one task left undone. A task he was going to complete today. Hopefully, it would end positively.

He knocked again.

Footsteps came pounding behind the door. "I'm coming, I'm coming!" an irritated female voice called out.

He tugged at his tie again, then shoved his hand in his pocket as the door opened a few inches. A head peeked around the corner, although the door continued to block the rest of her from his view.

He faced a woman he hadn't seen in years. By her choice. She had been more of a girl then. Her face had been rounder, hair longer and blonder. But he'd recognize the eyes of his baby sister anywhere.

"Aiden." One single word.

Was there hope in that tone? Would she slam the door closed on his face? She had the last time he'd tried to find her, right after she'd aged out of the foster care system. Back then, she'd been living with a boy she'd grown close to in the system. That was five years ago. Her gaze was shuttered now as she watched him. Wary. Had he imagined the hope?

The door moved slightly. He could now see her shoulders, which heaved as she sucked in a huge breath. They were too thin. When she exhaled, a sob came with it.

"Aiden," she said again, tears streaming down her face. "How did you find me?"

He wanted to reach out and pull her into a hug. But the door was still blocking him. Holding himself back, he tried to speak around the lump lodged firmly in the middle of his throat. It was difficult.

"I'm a cop. I have means." Cautiously he stepped closer. "Can we talk?"

She bit her lip, and for a moment he stopped breathing. She was going to say no. Then she took a step back and opened the door wider, gesturing for him to come in. He didn't give her a chance to change her mind. As he stepped past her, he realized that she was pregnant. Very pregnant.

Discreetly, he turned and looked at her left hand.

He let out a relieved sigh when he saw the wedding ring. She was married. Her baby would have a father.

He hoped the child would also be able to know his or her uncle. It all depended on how this visit turned out.

"Why don't we sit in the kitchen? I can make coffee. Or maybe you'd prefer a soda or water?"

"Water would be great." He followed her through to the kitchen. The apartment was small, but immaculate. And the furniture, though not the most expensive, was in good condition. When she opened the freezer to pull out an ice cube tray, he saw that it was well stocked. His anxiety lowered another notch. His sister wasn't wealthy, but she was married, in a good home and was no longer hungry. It meant a lot.

He seated himself at the table she indicated and waited. Now that he was here, all the practiced words flew out of his head. Instead, he watched her plink four ice cubes into a glass and fill it with water from a fil-tered pitcher.

It was only when she was seated across from him that he spoke.

"I've missed you, Jen. How are you?"

She smiled. That nearly killed his self-control right there.

"I'm good. Well, I'll be much better when this guy is born." She patted her belly gently. "It's strange that you showed up today. I have been thinking about you a lot lately. I saw you on the news a month or so ago. It said you were a murder suspect."

"That's been solved. I'm a cop. I was undercover, and my cover was blown."

"Figured it was something like that. I knew you wouldn't have murdered someone. You've always been too obsessed with doing the correct thing." She paused, her eyes zeroing in on his face. "I wanted to contact you, but couldn't work up the courage."

He reared back in surprise.

She noted his reaction. "Yeah, I knew that I was wrong five years ago to send you away. But I was feeling angry and broken."

He understood that. Hadn't he confessed being in that same condition to Sophie? Merely thinking of Sophie left his mind reeling with longing. The memory of her voice, the touch of her hand and the scent of strawberries had lingered and sustained him through the past few weeks apart.

"Does that mean you've forgiven me?" he asked Jennie quietly.

Her gaze dropped. "You never needed to be forgiven, Aiden. But I'm hoping you might forgive me?"

"Forgive you? What have you ever done that was wrong?"

"Oh, lots." She grinned, a flash that was there and gone. "But seriously, I was horrible to you. And you didn't deserve that. What have you ever done except try to help me?"

"He hurt you."

Even now, he couldn't bring himself to verbally say the name of their stepfather out loud.

"Yeah. He did. But he hurt you, too."

And their mother had been too scared to leave him. So they had survived the best they could.

An awkward silence fell between them. He tried to find a new topic of conversation. When she rubbed her stomach, he latched on to the subject of her coming baby.

"So, you're going to be a mom soon. When?"

Relief flared in her expression. "My due date is in three weeks."

He saw a picture wall. Jennie was standing with a tall man with lots of curly blond hair on a beach. They were smiling widely with their arms around each other. Their joy leaped off the picture.

He got up to take a closer look.

"This your husband?"

She didn't answer at first. He turned to see tears in her eyes. "Yes, that's Luke. We took that picture a year ago. He was killed six months ago in an explosion at the plant where he worked."

"Jennie." He didn't hold back this time. He marched up to her and gently hauled her into his arms. "I'm so sorry."

She didn't resist. His arms wrapped around her as much as her stomach would allow. He rubbed her back as she cried. When she stopped, he let her go.

"Jennie, I'm not going away again. I'm going to be your big brother and help you out."

She was already shaking her head. "I want you in

my life. But you don't need to protect me anymore. I'm a grown woman. I'll be fine."

"Maybe. But I'm still here for you. Whatever you need."

The tension had dissolved. They had many years of burdens to share. Jennie cried again when she learned of his time as a soldier. And again when he spoke of the death of his partner and the darkness of his under-cover work to find Tim's killer. "I'd wondered why you were gone so long."

"I had a lot to work through. Sophie helped."

Oh, no. He hadn't meant to tell her about Sophie. That was private. And it was also fragile. Sophie might not want him back, not after he'd left so abruptly.

The damage was done. Now that Jennie knew about Sophie, she peppered him with a thousand eager ques-tions. He answered briefly at first, but soon his longing for Sophie broke through his hesitance, and his words were tripping over each other as he talked about the woman who owned his heart.

"What are you doing here?" Jennie demanded.

"Huh?" he stared at his sister, confused.

"Don't get me wrong, I'm pleased as punch to see you. Ecstatic, really. But you obviously love this woman. Are you going to let her get away?"

"I needed to get us worked out first. Family is im-portant."

"It is." She looked at him thoughtfully. "When do I get to meet her?"

If only it was that simple!

"I don't know." He shook his head. "I don't know

if she'll want anything to do with me. I didn't exactly leave in the best way."

"So?" She slammed her fists on her hips and glared. "Fight for her. Fight with her, if necessary. Love is worth it. You don't have time to waste. Trust me. And when—not if—she accepts you, savor every moment you have together."

He saw the picture of her husband again and understood the message.

"I will, sis. I will."

"Good." Jennie wrote out her cell phone number and handed it to him. When he had put it in his pocket, she shoved him toward the door. "Go get your woman. Call me when you have a wedding date set."

"Is this Sophie?"

Sophie frowned. She didn't recognize the woman's voice. It was light and pleasing. Probably a telemarketer or a scam. She should hang up without answering.

Except, it might be someone at Celine's deaf camp calling her. Celine had waffled about whether or not she should attend the yearly camp. The recent events had given her nightmares.

Sophie had discussed the pros and cons with her, but had let Celine make her own decision. In the end, Celine had opted to go after Sophie had promised her that a phone call would bring her to the camp immediately to bring her home if she wanted.

That was yesterday. Celine had called last night to talk with Sophie. Sophie had been amazed that she had braved the first night away.

"Hello?"

She was still holding the phone. "This is Sophie. Who is this? Please?"

She tacked the *please* on so the response wouldn't sound quite so rude.

There was a brief pause. "Um, do you have a sister named Celine?"

Sophie was instantly alarmed. Had something happened at camp? Was her sister hurt? "Yes, she's my sister. Is she all right?"

The woman on the phone sighed. "Finally. Do you know how many Sophie Larsons there are listed in the white pages?"

So it wasn't someone from camp. It was someone who had looked her up. Why? A thought occurred to her, and she almost dropped the phone as her heart raced. Maybe something had happened to Aiden.

"Who are you?"

"My name is Jennie Beiler. My maiden name is Forster."

She froze. Aiden's sister. Something had happened to him. Visions of him hurt or worse pushed into her mind. She sank onto the closest chair, unable to remain standing.

"Aiden. What's happened to Aiden?" she choked out. *Dear Lord, please let him be okay. Please.*

"He's fine. Really." The woman hurried to reassure her. "I didn't mean to scare you. Maybe I shouldn't have called. It's just…"

Her voice petered out.

"Jennie? It's just what? Why are you calling me?"

Aiden was fine. She said he was fine. She held on to those words, needing them to be true.

"Look, he came to see me. After all these years apart, he found me. And we talked. Talked like we haven't since we were taken into foster care. One thing he talked about was a beautiful red-haired woman named Sophie and her sweet kid sister."

Aiden had told his sister about her? That was hard to believe, although clearly he had. For what purpose?

"I'm surprised he mentioned me," she murmured.

Jennie laughed softly. "Well, to be honest, I don't think he planned to. But once he mentioned you, he couldn't seem to stop. The thing is, I'm pretty sure he's on his way to see you. And I'm hoping you'll listen to him."

Her heart thudded, the blood pounding in her ears, nearly drowning out Jennie's words.

"He's coming to see me."

She repeated the words, reluctant to believe. She couldn't take the disappointment if she was wrong.

She had suffered so much devastation recently. The investigation following the death of Phillip Larson had revealed that he had indeed been responsible for the deaths of their parents and Brian. It appeared her dad had discovered his brother's activities and had been preparing to turn him in. When her family's home had been searched, they had discovered that Phillip had planted bugs and had been listening in on her family for years.

One positive discovery was that, after she and Celine had been rescued, the doctor who'd been missing had been found. He'd been shot and left for dead, but he had survived. And he had been more than willing to testify against Phillip's men who had attacked him.

"Don't sound so surprised. Look, I can't tell you what to do. It's just that five years ago I sent him away, and I regretted it ever since. I'd been blaming him for all the ugliness in my life since we were placed in the foster care system as kids. I wanted to save him, and you, the same regret. If I could."

A motorcycle pulled into her driveway. She pushed the blind aside. Tears and joy mingled as the familiar features of the man they were talking about blurred. He set his helmet on the handlebars and faced the window. When he saw her watching him, a blazing smile spread across his face. She melted.

"Jennie. He's here."

"Go."

The phone disconnected. It slipped from her nervous hands. She didn't look as it hit the carpet. She didn't remember walking to the door. When she opened it, he was standing there, his gaze devouring her. She couldn't speak. His face was leaner than it had been.

"Hi, Soph."

"Hi." Brilliant response. She cleared her throat. "I just got off the phone with your sister."

His eyebrows climbed his forehead. "How'd she get your number?"

She told him about their conversation.

"I hope you weren't mad that she looked you up."

Was she angry? No. Confused. Fighting hope. Nervous. But not mad.

"Why did you tell her about me, Aiden?"

He shoved his hands into his pockets. She recognized that posture. He was feeling tense and trying to appear in control. She understood.

"I shouldn't have left like I did."

That wasn't exactly what she wanted to hear. Her fragile heart cracked a little. Maybe his sister had misunderstood. Maybe he wasn't regretting leaving her, just the way it had happened. Immediately, her defenses struggled to reassert themselves.

"How should you have left? You were very clear that we had no future. If I hadn't said…" She bit her lip. The last thing she wanted him to recall was what she had said to him. Her face heated, giving her one more reason to be irritated. She probably resembled a tomato right now with her red face.

His eyes widened. "No! That's not what I meant! I regretted leaving, period. Even while I was telling you all that, I knew I was lying! Both to you and to myself. I wanted a future with you. I still do. I just had stuff to fix first."

Her breath caught in her throat. Hope blossomed. She ignored the way spirals of giddiness were shooting through her veins. She couldn't let down her guard. Not yet. "You want a future with me?"

He reached out and took her hands in his. The thrill of having him here, touching her, nearly made her faint.

"Sophie Larson, I am absolutely, completely and forever in love with you. When you said you loved me, I got scared."

"Scared? Of what?"

He leaned down so their foreheads were touching. Her lids fluttered closed.

"I was terrified I'd fail you like I'd failed my sister."

"Aiden, you didn't fail her." Her right hand left his and crept up to rest against his cheek. He turned and kissed her palm.

When he straightened again, he kept hold of her left hand. "I know that now. She and I have reconciled. And I realized that I need to treasure the gift God has given to me. The gift of the love of a beautiful woman. And hopefully that of a family."

A family? She tightened her grip on his hand.

"Are you going to kiss her?"

Startled, they both turned to see they had a small audience. Six teenagers, an equal mix of male and female, were standing on the sidewalk, watching avidly. The girls were whispering and giggling, phones out.

Aiden tossed them a grin. "I'm getting to it."

Before she could respond, he went down on one knee. "Sophie Larson, I love you and want to spend my life with you and be a brother to Celine. Will you marry me?"

Sniffing, she nodded. "Oh, Aiden, I love you, too. Yes, yes, a thousand times yes, I'll marry you."

The kids on the sidewalk started cheering and clapping. Aiden jumped to his feet and pulled his new fiancée into his arms. When he leaned close, she welcomed his kiss and all the love he was offering. He broke the kiss long enough to whisper that he loved her and then recaptured her lips. She gave herself up to the joy, forgetting about their audience.

When they broke apart, she laughed. All six teenagers were holding out their phones.

"Did you guys record that?" she called out.

All six nodded.

"You want me to send you a copy?" one asked.

She normally wouldn't share her email, but this one time she made an exception.

"I'll bet that Jennie will want to see that," Aiden remarked.

"So will Celine."

He looked around. "Speaking of Celine, where is she?"

"She's at deaf camp this week."

Celine would be disappointed to miss this. "I think we should take a short trip and tell her. She's going to want to be my maid of honor."

He gave her the crooked grin she adored. "And Levi will want to be best man."

"Levi! He's okay?"

He nodded. "He's great. I talked with him last week. He knows I was coming here to propose. He said he'd get his bishop's approval to attend the wedding."

"Wait. His bishop?" This was new.

"After his stay with the King family, he realized that he belonged in the Amish world. He traveled to Berlin to reconcile with his family. It's not official yet, but he is hoping to join the Amish church in the near future."

She thought about that. "I'm happy for him." She leaned up and kissed his cheek.

"I agree. I can't wait to see my future sister. And to start planning our wedding."

Neither could she. As they strode to her car, he captured her hand and dropped a soft kiss on it.

She couldn't wait to begin their life together.

EPILOGUE

Sophie set down her paintbrush and stood back to admire her work. She'd never tried to stencil a border before, but decided she liked the look of it. It was time-consuming, true, but in her mind she envisioned what the completed room would look like. The slate blue walls were matte, which created a softer look. She sighed happily. It would be gorgeous when she was done. She couldn't wait for Aiden to see it.

"Sophie?"

She glanced at her watch. He was home early. Eagerly she turned toward the door.

"Back here, Aiden," she called.

Within seconds, he entered the room, his grin breaking across his handsome face like the sunrise. "Looks good."

Her heart sped up as she watched his face. They'd married three months after he'd returned and had been married for almost five months now, and she still couldn't believe he was hers. The man she'd almost given up on was standing beside her in the house they were building together. He turned and his eyebrow shot up as he caught her staring. She flushed, but flashed an answering smile at his crooked grin. He'd told her several times that he still felt the urge to reach out and touch her just to make sure she was real.

God had truly blessed them.

"I brought the paint you wanted." He gave the room a once-over. "Maybe I picked up the wrong color. It doesn't look like it would match the color scheme you've picked out for this room."

She swallowed her grin, joy bursting inside her like a water balloon hitting the ground. She ducked her head, busying herself with arranging the stencils so he wouldn't see the expression on her face.

"It's not for this room. I had an idea for the extra room next to ours."

"Oh?"

She pulled out the stencil she'd hidden at the bottom of the pile. It was an ABC stencil, in large bubble letters.

She held her breath.

He looked at it for a single moment, uncomprehending. Then she saw the knowledge flickering across his face. His dark eyes shimmered briefly before he blinked.

"Sophie." He cleared his throat, smoothing out the emotional edges in his voice. "Sophie, are you trying to tell me—"

"Does he know?" Celine burst into the room, shouting.

She skidded to a stop before them, her hazel gaze shooting between them. They both smiled at the way the thirteen-year-old was bouncing on the balls of her feet.

"I think your sister was just about to tell me something."

Both pairs of eyes focused on Sophie with laser precision.

"Well?" Celine demanded.

"Yes, Aiden. You're going to be a father."

He whooped and grabbed her in a hug, lifting her feet off the floor. She wrapped her arms around his neck and squeezed. After a couple of seconds, he lowered her back down but didn't release her. She buried her face in his neck, breathing in the woodsy scent that was all him.

"Still here, you know."

Celine's sarcasm broke them apart. She didn't appear upset. More amused.

"When, do you know?" Aiden asked.

"Sometime in the fall. The best I can figure is mid-October. I'll need to go to the doctor to get a better estimate."

"I'll be in school then," Celine mused. "Eighth grade starts end of August."

"Yes, but you're not going to be living away from home, so you'll still be here every evening to see your niece or nephew."

Celine nodded, content. "Can I call Aunt Jennie?"

Aiden glanced at Sophie, eyebrows raised. She and Jennie had become close friends in the past few months.

"Can you wait a few minutes?" Sophie asked. "We'll tell her the news together."

"Fine. I'm going to set up the computer so we can Skype."

Celine skipped from the room. It was so good to see her happy.

After everything that had happened, Celine had struggled with whether or not she wanted to return to the school for the deaf. She was terrified of being away from home, away from her sister, all week. Sophie no longer wanted to live in Chicago. Also, Aiden wanted to be near his sister, Jennie, and his new nephew. Jennie had named her son Luke after his dad. Everyone called the adorable little boy LJ. Aiden had been away from her for so long. When he and Sophie had found a house in a quiet part of Somerset County, Pennsylvania, they had made an offer the same day. It was close enough to the Western Pennsylvania School for the Deaf to enroll Celine as a day student, so she could still attend a school where everyone signed but would come home every day.

And they were able to see Jennie and LJ every weekend. It was perfect.

Celine would get impatient soon. Aiden helped Sophie pack away her painting supplies for the day, and then they made the phone call to Jennie. As expected, Jennie was over the moon for her brother and Sophie. She promised to help them decorate the baby's room and pick out furnishings.

After the call ended, Sophie and Aiden walked out to sit on the deck he'd built at the back of the house. On the way there, he grabbed the iced coffee he'd picked up for his wife on the way home. Caramel with whipped topping, complete with caramel drizzle. Her heart melted. Her husband knew her well. She waited for him as he nipped over to the refrigerator and grabbed a Dr Pepper for himself. Together, they settled into the wicker love seat she'd fallen in love with, holding hands as they enjoyed their beverages and each other's company.

"A baby." He leaned his head back and smiled. "Jennie's kid will have a playmate."

"Well, there will be a small age difference. How'd your day go?" Sophie licked a glob of caramel and whipped topping off her straw before sipping the coffee itself. Cold, sweet and delicious. Life was good.

"It was good. I had a few sophomores and juniors, but most of the students were freshmen."

She listened carefully for any hint of discontent and was relieved when she heard none. When they had moved, he'd put out feelers to old contacts and had been immediately contacted by a former captain, asking if he'd be willing to take a position as an instructor at the police academy. They'd prayed hard about it.

Sophie would never have asked him to step away from a career he loved, and he knew it.

"Are you happy you took the position?"

"Absolutely." Not a second of hesitation. "You know I'll tell you if I want to return to the field, but I was burned-out. It was time to try something new."

A sigh left her. He put his soda on the table beside him.

"Hey, what's that sigh for?" His thumb rubbed her palm, sending goose pimples up her arm.

"Nothing." She leaned her head on his strong shoulder. "I'm just so happy here."

She moved her head to gaze up at him. He wrapped

his arms around her, smiled and leaned down, erasing the distance between them. Just before their lips met, he whispered, "Me, too. I have everything I need, right here in my arms."

He kissed her, telling her without words that she was precious and beloved.

* * * * *

If you enjoyed this book, don't miss the other heart-stopping Amish adventures from Dana R. Lynn's Amish Country Justice series:

Plain Target
Plain Retribution
Amish Christmas Abduction
Amish Country Ambush
Amish Christmas Emergency
Guarding the Amish Midwife
Hidden in Amish Country

Find more great reads at www.LoveInspired.com.

Dear Reader,

I am so thrilled to be able to share Aiden and Sophie's story with you. The idea of an undercover police officer who breaks his cover to protect someone has been in my mind for a while now. I especially wondered how he would suffer being immersed in his cover, like Aiden was. Aiden is wounded by all that he suffered, but he still held tight to his faith, which carried him through.

Sophie has allowed her faith to slide, but the danger she finds herself in helps her remember what is truly important. And having a handsome protector didn't hurt, either.

A bonus for me was adding in the character of Celine, Sophie's younger sister, who is deaf. She won my heart, and I hope she touched yours, as well.

I love hearing from readers! I can be found on Facebook and Instagram, or you can contact me through my website at www.danarlynn.com.

Blessings,
Dana R. Lynn

COMING NEXT MONTH FROM
Love Inspired Suspense
Available July 7, 2020

EXPLOSIVE SITUATION
True Blue K-9 Unit: Brooklyn • by Terri Reed
Detective Henry Roarke's determined to prove his innocence to internal affairs officer Olivia Vance—but first he must survive the bomber targeting him and his bomb-sniffing K-9. Olivia plans to keep close tabs on Henry, but with his life on the line, can they make it out alive?

AMISH SANCTUARY
by Katy Lee
When someone comes after one of her counseling patients, Naomi Kemp promises to shield the woman's baby. Now with a murderer on her tail, Naomi flees back to the Amish roots—and the ex-fiancé—she left behind. But can Sawyer Zook save her and the child as Naomi faces her traumatic past?

GUARDED BY THE SOLDIER
Justice Seekers • by Laura Scott
After months of searching for missing pregnant single mother Olivia Habush and her young son, former special ops soldier Ryker Tillman finally tracks them down—just as they are attacked by armed mercenaries. Protecting Olivia, her unborn child and little Aaron is Ryker's new mission, but who wants them dead?

HUNTED BY THE MOB
by Elisabeth Rees
An assignment turns deadly when FBI agent Goldie Simmons has a bounty placed on her head. Now relying on her long-lost childhood sweetheart, Zeke Miller—the fellow agent originally slated to be her partner on the case—is her only hope of survival as the mafia hunts her down.

FOLLOWING THE EVIDENCE
by Lynn Shannon
Moving to Texas to claim her inheritance is supposed to be a new beginning for widowed single mother Emma Pierce—until someone tries to kill her. But Sheriff Reed Atkinson won't let anything happen to his first love...especially when he finds out her case may be tied to his sister's disappearance.

ROCKY MOUNTAIN REVENGE
by Rhonda Starnes
Temporarily home as interim veterinarian at her late father's clinic, Grace Porter has no intentions of staying—but someone's dead set on guaranteeing she doesn't live long enough to leave. With both Grace and her sister in a killer's crosshairs, it's up to her ex-boyfriend, police chief Evan Bradshaw, to guard them.

LISCNM0620